TWO

THE TRILOGY OF WISHBONE HOLLOW

CAP

FULL OF

DREAMS

A NOVEL OF HISTORICAL FICTION

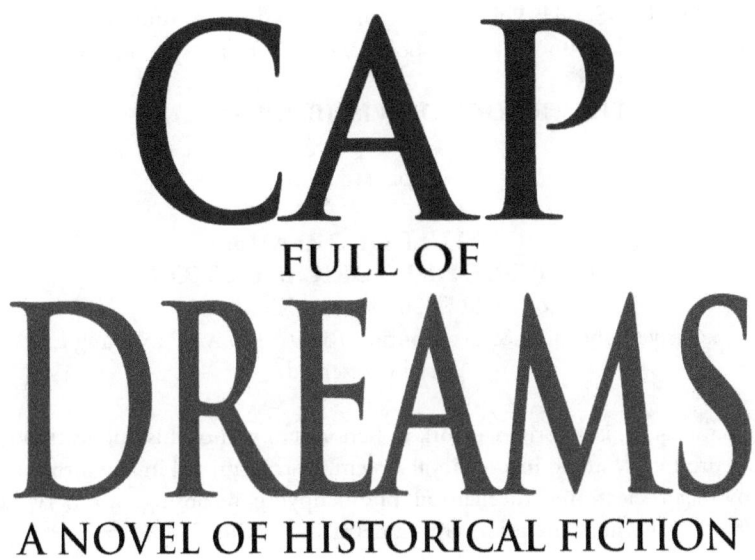

JOANN KLUSMEYER

innovo
PUBLISHING

Published by Innovo Publishing, LLC
www.innovopublishing.com
1-888-546-2111

Providing Full-Service Publishing Services for Christian Authors, Artists &
Ministries: Books, eBooks, Audiobooks, Music, Screenplays, Film & Curricula

THE TRILOGY OF WISHBONE HOLLOW

Volume 2

CAP FULL OF DREAMS:
A NOVEL OF HISTORICAL FICTION
Copyright © 2023 Joann Klusmeyer
Exclusive Publishing & Distribution Rights: Innovo Publishing LLC
All rights reserved.

ISBN: 978-1-61314-748-1

Cover Design & Interior Layout: Innovo Publishing, LLC

Printed in the United States of America
U.S. Printing History
First Edition: 2023

Has God called you to create a Christian book, ebook, audiobook, music album,
screenplay, film, or curricula? If so, visit the ChristianPublishingPortal.com to
learn how to accomplish your calling with excellence. Learn to do everything
yourself, or hire trusted Christian Experts from our Marketplace to help.

CONTENTS

BACKGROUND

Writ by Herman Jones from over to Stony Point.

I t sorta fell to me to catch events up to date. Little old Wishbone Holler, from upper Arkansas, rocked along into 1916 with a few important changes.

Europe was rumbling toward a war and those of us on the "spit and whittle bench" figgered good old U.S.A. would be pulled into a war and hopin' we was wrong. I used to come over to Wishbone while Irvin Hopkins was a'preachin' at the church, but him and me, we both got too old. It was a big change for him, but he was holdin' up fairly well till that granddaughter from up the hill got big enough to start tryin' to find her own way.

That thirteenth kid'a the Moffat's made a lotta conversation in town when she rescued the two kidnapped persons and wounded the kidnapper. After that, she was called on to sit with a coupla'a measles patients and she did herself proud, it seems. That should'a told old Irwin that the fourteen-year-old girl they called Rowenna was headed out on her own path where old granddad wouldn't be able to follow, and maybe he knew it but it was like takin' the actual breath outta his lungs to even think on it.

Not only that, his old yeller horse he calls Mustard hung his head over the fence waitin' on that girl to come and ride 'im into the mountains...and she don't come. Old Irvin has answers to 'er questions when she asks, but the girl seems to findin' 'er own way. Bein' two hollers away don't help none, but baby birds leave the nest and youngens leave to wherever they have to go. It was sort'a agreed on, here at the "bench," that the youngen a his was goin' far. So far, she's only goin' over to Eureka, but that's just the start.

We read the papers and some of us listen to our radio sets and we see the straws in the wind of the storm comin' on, and we'll get pulled into it, sure as God made puckery green persimmons. Squabbles in Europe is gonna mean bloodshed in America. We look at our girls fillin' marriage chests and boys practicin' their sparkin' words, and we wonder how the war'll mess up their efforts.

We were decades later findin' the remains'a the fellows in the war of the brothers. Those young fellows were aimin' to do their own sparkin', too, but it didn't happen for 'em. The whole world knows what DID happen.

Most of us are thinkin' we're right there at that same place again. Old men make war and young men die. Looks like a few women might die alongside. So we sit on the bench and talk about the weather…bein' we can't stand to think on anything else. The only thing to solace old Irvin is that the light of his life can shoot a gun, and he was the one to make sure it was possible. Could be it'll save 'er life…again.

So sit back and watch with us, if you will. You'll notice that where we refer to somethin' from the Bible, we marked with an asterisk (*).

(Every part of this book is fiction, and there is no resemblance intended toward any person, living or dead.)

CAP FULL OF DREAMS

ROWENNA MOFFAT, ON HER OWN

And there she stood, a sixteen-year-old girl…poised to step into the rest of her life with her whole insides trembling like a willow leaf in a storm.

She did not have to take this step…in fact, there were those who would have begged her to turn around while there was time. To go home where she was loved. But those who would have told her that also knew their words would be useless.

She was, however, under control of an inner force…a force that is in every human who will permit it. She bravely stepped inside the large white building in Eureka Springs and looked around. For some reason she instantly felt at home. How could that possibly be?

Armed with the Gold Certificate earned in her hilltop home, she had proof that she had mastered all current rules and regulations toward cleanliness and care, first aid to accident victims, best procedures during epidemics, and skill in the easing of fear of the frightened. She had read about how to administer medical preparations and determine the extent of their effectiveness.

She did not, however, have enough years of age to actually enter the nursing school as a student. There were the "blue caps," though, and they were the hospital volunteers…those either too young, or for some other reason wished to see what nurses did before actually starting the classes.

Rowenna was happy to be a blue cap. She had already passed the classes, and she wanted only to see those things done that she had read about.

Old Midwife Gardener wasn't so sure. Here a sixteen-year-old child was going to be put with her to observe. Now what did that mean? No matter. She would do what she had to so…and that was bringing babies into the world…all in one piece and breathing.

Nurse Bennett was of an opposite opinion. "Why I'd be glad to have that girl on my team. I was barely big enough to peek over the edge of the table when I first started watchin' my pa. He learned sewin' human bodies together durin' the war. Him out there with nothin' to work with 'cept his sewin' kit and other young fellows bleedin' out on the ground, what was he to do? He learned…that's what.

"That there battle'a Pea Ridge over to the west, and it was one'a the worse. It was on those ridges that two armies met and neither hardly knew what it was all about…'cept being pushed on by their feather-brained officers sent out from the east. The hills and caves of Arkansas ain't no place for a civilized war. That battle was more like two roosters fightin' in a pit, and the one that didn't get killed now was gonna be made to fight again and killed later.

"My Pa, he got to thinkin' his best war effort was to patch up the fellows best he could, no matter what color'a uniform they wore. That war bein' waged right there in our cow pasture made it handy for him to get a lot of practice. Word got around that if you could get a wounded fellow back to the Bennett cave, he'd be took care of.

"Sure thing. You let that girl work with me and don't make her sit through classes she'd done had when she can learn a lot by just lookin' on. Good chance I might need somethin' like hot water and she'd be there to get it."

So Rowenna was welcomed into what was called surgery. Sewing up wounds seemed so exciting, her eyes danced with anticipation. One had to wait, however, until a problem happened to get to see how it was fixed.

The "layin-in" hospital and nursing school was a four storied frame structure on the edge of the small Arkansas city of Eureka Springs. The idea of that nursing school had its birth in an old Civil War Hospital set up in the Crescent Cave. Later it was called the Crescent Hospital, but after a few bouts of organizational "labor pains" it outgrew its cave and began its growth in the huge frame building. The nursing school began by being held together from the sheer force of determination of a few strong-minded civic women.

This school was badly needed. Everyone agreed. There was no way a doctor or even a pair of doctors could adequately care for the scattered farmhouses perched on the hillsides. There needed to be "after care" of illnesses and that was impossible for a doctor to provide...and generally the patient did not actually need the services of a doctor by then...only a few days of rest to regain strength. This was best done with a skilled person to administer any medical preparations.

The first floor of the building housed the emergency room and the offices of the administrators. Its ground floor also had an add-on for the kitchen and a serving bar for dining. Second floor was for the patients requiring bed-care and the third was for specialized equipment, quarantine requirements and the delivery room. The fourth floor under the attic was for the nurses. It was decided that fifty beds could be set up, though that made them very close together. Parts of the attic were curtained off with sheets to provide a bit of privacy for the fifty girls.

The plan was that the course would last one year, from January on to December. The first six months would have the students in morning classes, and the afternoons would for hands on, though there was a lot of room for flexibility. Later it was changed to the more practical method of dividing the girls into groups of twenty-five, starting a second class beginning in July and lasting to the last of June.

This plan only worked on paper, because any girl could be pulled for any purpose at any hour, and night duty was an important part of the education. If the girl could not function without her eight hours of sleep every night, perhaps she was not cut out to be a nurse. It made sense, actually.

In addition to the regular students, there were the blue cap volunteers…being anywhere from one to six in number. They were a fluid group, many of them deciding after the first week that nursing was not their "cup of tea," so to speak, and they would be gone.

The regular uniform was white, covered by a white coverall apron. Comfortable shoes…they hoped…with a three quarter-inch heel. The skirts were gathered enough to provide ease in walking, and they reached a modest six inches below the knee. A hip-length cape of lined broadcloth would guard against chill when it was necessary for them to step outside in the winter.

Beds were thirty inches wide and constructed of local lumber with a woven rope mesh under the mattress (tick) of goose feathers. The attic was rather one of the warmest of the floors in the winter, and all-wool blankets were issued when necessary.

To some girls, this seemed rather Spartan, but to many, it was even more luxurious than they had at home. Each girl had her own bed, and that was a valued gift. No matter, certainly, that the next bed was only twelve to eighteen inches away. Some schools had actually slept three to the bed.

The first-floor dining area comfortably sat twenty and the various groups were scheduled…more or less…for their meals. This was approximate as any girl could be pulled at any time and be advised she could eat later. Just more good practice for what would happen when she had a real job.

The community was generous in sharing food with the school. One of the few things the mountain farms had in overabundance, was food. Potatoes, both white and sweet, onions, turnips, and winter squash being the favorites for donation. Tomatoes in season and melons were favorites. There were those who would can their extra tomatoes for the school, asking only to "trade out" jars so they would have some containers for next year.

A gift of a dressed-out, butchered calf, hog, sheep or goat was not unusual, and made a good protein addition. Dry beans and peas were a staple, and cornmeal for bread and rolled oats for breakfast porridge was often donated. Food was simple and somewhat monotonous, but the girls were there to learn…not to eat. Donated supplies kept costs down and skilled cooks made use of what was available.

Rowenna was taken aside by the supervisor, Mrs. Florence Cameron. This sixteen-year-old created a separate category, and it was well she learn that from the first.

She gave Rowenna the tag to pin to her dress that said, "R. MOFFAT" and settled her down at the big desk. "Now, Rowenna, I'm sure you know that you were accepted for reasons other than those of most blue caps. We here have had lengthy discussions and agree that you should not sit in a class to re-learn what you have learned already as proved by your Gold Seal Certificate. So, if you were put in a class, it would be unhandy to pull you from a class you have already completed to assist in something that you are here to learn. Another reason is that the other girls would wonder why you were different, and that would not be a good thing. We have almost a year and a half until you are eighteen, and I know you were counting on a white cap in January but that would be a mistake. Leaving you as a volunteer will keep you free to assist and learn while keeping the older girls from thinking you are receiving special treatment. Far from it! I might mention that this plan was suggested by my niece who signed your Certificate.

"So…you will be assigned a bed in the attic, but you will spend most nights, maybe all nights, on third floor with patients. Your locker will also be on the third floor. You will understand, I'm sure, that as a volunteer, there will be no fee for your "training." It would be a mistake to try to treat you like the other girls as none of them have taken and passed the courses of study you have.

"You were interested in midwifery, and so often babies choose to arrive in the night. You will be aroused from your bed to assist. So many accidents happen late in the afternoon, and if you can assist Nurse Bennett, you will be kept up as long as necessary…even all night. She has years of experience in handling everything from knife wounds to scald burns, to broken bones. We are of the opinion that is what you want to learn.

"If these rules sound too harsh, we would understand if you wished to withdraw, and perhaps return when you're older. That would be up to you. Volunteers often withdraw so no one would think less of you."

Mrs. Cameron paused, smiled and waited for a response.

"Oh, no…NO! Never! I tried too hard to get here. I like everything you said. I don't mind the blue cap…really. Besides, it matches the capes. I had to wake up at night with my sister's measles, and sometimes didn't get to sleep at all. And the little girl I helped…it was not a problem for me to be up with her."

The supervisor smiled, nodded assurance and was not surprised. "So we'll go and get your clothes, assign you a bed on both floors, give you a time to have your meals…assuming you are not busy at that time. If any of the girls ask why your bed and schedule are different…tell them, truthfully, you are too young to do anything else."

In the galley, the aroma of vegetable soup was strong and spicy. Leftover biscuits were being crumbled into a batter to make bread pudding. Apron clad cooks scurried around with their jobs.

Rowenna's new life had begun.

*Psalm 91: 11

GRANDDAD AND THE NEWSPAPERS

Here it was 1916 and the world was whizzing into its future like a burning comet. It was now highly possibly to have newspapers down at the Frisco depot that were not more than three days old, and often, just two days. They came from

Memphis, Tennessee; St Louis, Missouri; Kansas City and even Little Rock, Arkansas.

They contained a lot of words, but the ones that interested old Rev. Irvin Hopkins were the ones about Europe and the war. The old man was wrinkled and gray, but he was nobody's fool. He could read a word and understand its meaning.

He had been trained on the best of books, being the King James Version of the Holy Bible, and there were a lot of words in that book that took a lot of study to fully understand. There were other words that he could not understand at all, but he knew that when God expected that of him, he would help him to see the message clearly.

And now he had the newspapers. It paid to keep an eye on the European royalty as these ruling families were forever scuffling over turf possession, and the borders to the smaller counties were continually being shuffled this way and that.

One country that seemed to get the worse of the shuffle was Belgium, sometimes being called Flanders. This was located in what was called a "low country"…along with Netherlands and Luxemburg. Most of the people referred to themselves as Flemish, and spoke Dutch, French or a unique blend of both.

The French border pushed north, and the Dutch border pushed south as the Hollanders claimed more land from the water, and created peninsulas extending out into the ocean. It was the creation of these below-sea-level lands that gave Holland the name of "NETHER" lands.

When Granddad Hopkins studied the new maps that were published in the papers, he immediately saw the danger point. There was England across the channel and the distance from their closest point, Dover, to Europe's closest point, Calais, was about twenty and a half miles. Actually, there had been strong armed persons who had managed to actually swim across.

That width, in fact, would be the most valuable spot of land for Germany's purposes, and in the event of a war in Europe, England would of necessity be drawn in. That point of land would be the natural meeting place.

So when Granddad received the papers, he searched quickly for each new and updated map, and for words from both sides. Then he would sigh and take his place on the city's "spit and whittle" bench, so named for the activity used by once active fingers to keep themselves busy, and the propensity to chew toothpicks, thereby having hair-sized splinters in their mouths. Spitting was therefore required.

Over and over Granddad thought of his many grandsons… now married and starting their families. Reason told him that if America's brother country, England, got in a war, America would rush to help, as families did. And there was that mischief-maker in central Europe, called Prussia (or Germany) who must be watched.

There was the interesting fact that Queen Victoria of England was the grandmother of the Mischief-maker, called Wilhelm II. As a young man, Wilhelm greatly admired the English and spent vacations there, but as he began to rule Germany, he became jealous, and thought if he took over that island kingdom, then he could have it all. The best way to take it over was to over-run the small countries on the way. He planned a "great rush to the sea" and in the pathway was Belgium, and to an extent, Holland.

Granddad talked about the weather and visited with his friends on the bench, but his thoughts were on what was happening around the world…events that would affect his family of grandsons.

While back at his lonely house, he wondered about the light of his life, Rowenna, in whom so many of his dreams were centered, and on Wally, her cousin who would be poised to be conscripted into the army just about the time the war began. For the last two years, since 1914, the overseas bickering had accelerated, and now, with 1917 looming just ahead, there was cause for worry. Not that worry would help.

At least, Rowenna, being a girl, would be safe when war broke out…as it surely would. Little did he how of how events would shape the lives of his grandchildren. Especially the life of Rowenna.

And Rowenna, now two hollers away, met Dollie Duffy. When she first saw her, Dollie was outfitted in a dress of white and on her head was a stiffly starched cap that was meant to hold back her hair and also to indicate her status. Blue cap.

It was then that the Scheduler, Miss Osborn, called for Moffat and Duffy and handed them each a broom. The first floor was to be swept several times daily. Rowenna curiously peeked at her associate as they worked. About her age…maybe. It was hard to tell.

Her tag said D. Duffy. Her hair was as black as the coal that was hacked from the mountains, and her skin as pale as the paper on Miss Osborn's desk…or so it seemed. Eyes, dark as the onyx marbles valued by small boys, and lashes like shiny brushes, dark as half-past midnight. She was round-faced, short-nosed and sported a wide smile.

Together they pushed the floor dirt into a pile and removed it and were set about to folding sheets fresh from the laundry. Dollie, it seemed, came from a settlement called Cedar Bluff, and she was to be the great hope of that small, doctor-less community.

In subsequent conversations, Rowenna was to learn that the first half of her fee, being twenty-five dollars was earned partly from her own efforts and the rest from community gatherings called "pie suppers" where pennies were paid by fellows for the rights to eat with a certain girl. It was a well-used method of collecting community funds.

It was hoped that Dollie would return with her nursing education and skill to the community that needed this help. Dollie, herself, was terribly nervous and excited, but so happy to be there. She would be blue cap until January when the new class started, and her twenty-five dollar fee was paid until the end of June.

Beautiful Dollie could have been the "poster girl" of those young women who managed to find a way to get the nurse training at the schools like the one at Eureka Springs, Arkansas. The need was so great…and so well-known and deplored…that many communities were obliged to financially help a willing and educationally-advantaged girl, rather than sending a young man to be a doctor.

The midwifery benefit may have been the most important driver of this premise, but, fact be known, the obstacles put in the way of educating girls, along with the "hoops" they must jump through, winnowed out their numbers until they were left with Dollie, Rowenna and others like them, such as Marianna Stanton, Erma Melton and dozens of others. Girls who had a vision.

Determined, headstrong girls were found sprinkled throughout the ridges and hollows of Northern Arkansas. To most of them, it was never a need for power or community status... but an inborn desire to help humanity by alleviating pain. It was something they could do.

The laundry-folding job caused these two to miss the evening meal, an event that was to happen most of the time, and they appeared at the galley for leftovers with aching arms from the multitude of sheets and towels.

Soup. A standby for supper, along with cornbread or crackers, usually pickles or some kind of relish. Often a boiled egg rounded out the meal along with some kind of baked dessert. Today was bread pudding made from a custard base filled with broken leftover biscuits and baked. It was a favorite because there was usually seconds or maybe even thirds.

The girls found no complaint with the food, being ravenously hungry after the activity. Then, at lights-out (except for those on night duty) they retired to their separate beds. This brought up the question as to why Rowenna was bedded on the third floor, and Dollie with the other nurses on the fourth.

Fortunately, Mrs. Cameron had given her the answer to give. "Too young. I can't even be a white cap for a year and a half. I'm supposed to sleep down here."

There. That would spread the word around if there was any question.

And it was in the night that good-natured Mamie Johnson checked in for her fourth baby. It wasn't that she needed help... or anything. She knew the drill.

Having a baby was less painful for her than a sprained ankle, and certainly was over a lot quicker. She was here because she loved to be cared for, tea brought when she wanted it, and the new baby bathed and bedded elsewhere for two whole days. She left her husband at home with the other three and drove herself down to town. Her horse and buggy were put in the hospital livery at three in the afternoon, and she was put to bed at five pm, dilation having begun.

At eleven P.M., half of the July semester class was awakened to observe, and Rowenna was with them. She was permitted to stand aside and see what she wished she had known earlier in the year. There were really things that could be done to make the birth easier, though Mamie really didn't need them. She had this birthing job down pat.

Being of generous proportions, Mamie had, on previous visits, opted to use the birthing-chair. At this time, the general practice was for the midwife to station herself behind the mother when dilation reached a certain point. The assistant midwife held the woman at a thirty to forty-five degree angle which gave the baby a better exit slant. Or so it was thought.

There were, however, birthing stools with a slanted back and a seat with a circular opening for the ejection of the baby. This made the operation possible for one midwife to officiate. She would likely bring her own birthing-chair for the event. This allowed her to catch the baby from a frontal position.

This chair was optional at the laying-in hospital, and though most of the younger mothers chose the bed...or the flatness of the floor, Mamie liked the chair.

She laughed and joked with the nurses, and Midwife Gardner then settled herself in a padded easy chair and rested. At the proper moment, Mamie was assisted from the bed to the birthing-chair...her gown adjusted...and the student nurses gathered around.

A large bowl with blanket padding was placed under the chair, to make certain the baby would not land on the floor should it slip from the hands of the midwife. Truthfully, babies

19

were slick. This stool also made it possible for a woman to deliver at home...alone. The slant of the chair back insured the baby's decent would be safe.

For some reason, this wonderful apparatus had lost popularity about the late 1800's, but it fascinated Rowenna. If she'd had that with Emily Parnell, Emily would have had a much better time. Rowenna had been two years younger when that event had occurred unexpectedly and she had been alone...but what a wonderful apparatus this chair was!

And could her luck be even better...yes! This jolly lady was going to use it! That was when old Midwife Gardner demanded. "BLUE CAP! Get yourself back'a the chair and don't let that pan move a smidgeon from where I put it."

Rowenna jumped to attention and almost lost the blue cap from her head. Scurrying to the back of the birthing chair, she knelt and reached under the chair. Huh! Handles on the pan. Just in the right place. So this was a real job, assuming there were enough people in attendance. She crouched low so she could view the whole perimeter of the pan...eighteen inches in diameter, about. If that didn't catch all of the baby, it would have to be a terribly big kid!

The students gathered around, excited for Mamie...because Mamie was so excited for herself. Mrs. Gardner told her when to breath...as if she didn't know. Imagine that! Rowenna had never told Miss Emily when to breathe and she seemed to know what to do. Amazing.

Mrs. Gardner sternly demanded. "Big breath. Let it out. Another big breath and push."

Rowenna could see around Mamie that the six students were on their knees, also looking at the pan. It was a tiny disappointment when the pan remained uninterestingly empty. Mamie's little girl had slid obediently into the outstretched fingers of the midwife.

The midwife turned her head and demanded, "You...on the end. Come over here with the tray."

The startled girl scooted the prepared tray toward the midwife, who told her, "Now...do what you know to do." Apparently the student did what was demanded.

"Now...you over there," and she pointed with her elbow, "grab a towel and take the baby. You...next to her...go with her to bathe the baby the way I told you. The rest of you scoot closer to me and watch what comes next."

Then it was over, and with a small sigh of disappointment, Rowenna relaxed her death-grasp on the handles of the pan (without baby) and joined the students.

Then she and the students were sent to bed. But how could anyone ever go to sleep after all that excitement? But she was hardly back in her sleeping gown when someone said "Moffat! Up and start the day!" It was the voice of Miss Osborn, Scheduler, whose voice she was to hear frequently in the next months.

In the designated time of ten minutes, she was dressed, washed, hair coiled to fit under her cap and had arrived into the kitchen. A long-handled ladle was handed her to stir the porridge which was oatmeal this morning.

The she prepared trays for the patients. Oatmeal, sugar, buttered biscuit, garden tea. A peeled boiled egg in a separate small cup that just fit the egg. Small salt and pepper shakers were furnished. The nurses she had seen in the night were there to carry the trays.

In an hour it was finished, and she could have her own breakfast with whoever was free. So many new faces...how could she ever learn them all...but then she didn't have to.

Just follow orders. Dottie smiled and waved as she was carrying a pail of kitchen garbage out to the hogs who consumed it, and they, themselves, would later be consumed.

Rowenna was set about with the chamber pails, carrying the night soil of the patients to the privy. Only one flight of steps. The students had three flights to dispose of theirs.

One thing followed the other, and the day was over.

A DROP BACK TO BACK TO 1914

Granddad and the Spit and Whittle group (retired fellows who meet and discus, whittle and spit) had plenty to talk about while discussing just what happened right here in Wishbone, but the newspapers also had a lot of interesting information. Rowenna's Granddad was one of those who devoured news, and at that time a lot was happening that would have interested him if he had known.

It was thought by most of the locals that the Wright Brothers, in their own country of America, invented air travel, but the idea of mimicking the birds seemed to descend on humanity at about the same time all over the world. The French were working with various styles of airborne apparatuses. England had their goals and Germany was experimenting with inflated dirigibles that floated rather than flying on their own power. Brilliant German engineers were also prototyping various other designs of self-powered aircraft as well as explosives.

When the war was declared, it was not long before Germany managed to drop a few bombs on London…some creating massive potholes in the streets.

It was partly these potholes that spurred the activity in England to create something better to fight back with. They started from the absolute beginning, using for a pattern the "aero planes" that were essentially the toys of rich men's sons.

These broomstick and canvas toys could actually get into the air and were a source of "fun-danger" for young men on a Sunday afternoon…to fly over the acres of the manor house…to look down on the roofs of the rest of the world.

From the seeds of these beginnings the nation feverously began to experiment for something with more power. The small, engine-driven toys could actually be tipped over in a twenty mile per hour wind. Certainly they were not to be trusted to cross the channel, perform service, and have the reserve power to return.

There needed to be aircraft to combat the dirigibles carrying German explosives, and perhaps even more…the ability to see where the enemy actually was. Up until now the limit of surveillance was the distance the eye could see from the position he managed to get himself. Scouts were used to forge ahead and hopefully return with information the commanders could use... that is, if they could keep themselves from being killed.

Engineers and tinkerers worked industriously for improvement to this light aircraft, and there were small successes. It seemed possible that there would soon be a way to circle out over the Dover cliffs and cross the channel, to peer down with telescopes and attempt to guess the next action of the enemy. To see well, however, the plane must swoop low, and the lack of speed made them a perfect target for ground fire.

Not good. A position must be carved out across the channel into the tiny country of Belgium for a place to land the plane if necessary, and take off again in hopes of gaining the needed information. That worked better except for one thing.

The promontory called Ypres (English pronunciation: I-per). This was Belgium's nearest point to England and in the direct path of the German emperor, Kaiser Wilhelm, and his announced "race to the sea." The English knew that his "race was to the sea" was another word for race to "conquer England."

What followed was the bloodiest battle of all wars of the time. The armies worked from trenches, the warring sides often as near as a mile apart. It was absolutely necessary to be up high enough to see what was going on in the enemy trenches and be fast enough to escape bullets from the ground. This problem plagued both armies almost equally and forced the race for who controlled the air.

And then there was Kaiser Wilhelm who ruled Germany. This man was half English...his grandmother being Queen Victoria. He was even named after her...Frederick Wilhelm Viktor (after Victoria) Albrecht of Prussia.

As a child, he was proud of his English heritage but was encouraged by military leaders such as Otto Von Bismarck to hate the English and that influenced him to decide to take over that country by force.

Granddad Hopkins knew some of this...enough to be concerned. He also knew of the experimental planes that shot their weapons forward, trusting that the bullet would not hit a wing of the propeller on the way. It was not a comforting thought that it was actually possible to shoot themselves down. He sought through the papers for more information, but it seemed that the mid-American newspapers were not long on the subject.

The problem of the war was a great distance away...across an ocean...and Granddad Hopkins was in middle America. His last two grandchildren, Rowenna and Wally, were seen daily around town. It was this year that Rowenna's gun helped to catch a kidnapper and manage the release of a woman and a baby. He was put behind bars for life.

That same girl battled with a desire to become a nurse...like Florence Nightingale...but the family members were certain it was just a little girl's dream because she had read about the brave nurse of the Crimean war.

The family was wrong, it would seem later, as the girl managed to get the books that nurses study from even though she was still years underage for the school. And now she had a Certification of Completion...and not only that...hers had a Gold Seal of Excellence!

So the girl's most dependable source of encouragement was Granddad and the angel (angels...?) promised to her by God in Psalm 91:11. It was very encouraging to know one had the help of the angel who was "given charge over her" to "keep her." So the girl just kept doing what was ahead of her that seemed possible to do, and now she found herself in an actual hospital with actual teachers to train her.

That was then...and now year 1916 was coming to a close, and the sixteen-year-old girl was facing another birthday...her seventeenth.

THE BATTLES WITH THE NO-SEE-EMS

As far back as ancient Egypt it was known that there were invisible forces that attempted to thrive in human bodies, eventually destroying their host. It was also known that some humans continued to live in spite of the invisible invasion and when that happened, certain no-see-ems no longer had power over that person.

This was wonderful knowledge if they could just figure out what to do with it. All the way from huts to castles this war against the no-see-ems was waged. There is evidence of humans burning such vegetation as pine and cedar, eucalyptus and other aromatics in attempt to kill or at least drive away what they could not see. This was met with negligible success, except to make the huts and caves smell better. Maybe.

They learned, also, that simple smoke killed organisms in meat and fish making storage possible without spoiling, and even smoke was attempted against these no-see-ems. This was to no avail that anyone could see....

It took a Japanese biologist teaming up with German organization to isolate the origin of Tetanus (or what they locally called "Lockjaw"). To them, it made sense that if some humans could survive the invasion, then part of that person might be injected into another person and help him survive. Hence vaccine made an appearance.

It took the late 1800's to begin to make this knowledge available to everyone, and even longer to make the vaccine ready to use. A lot was still unknown, but they did know that lockjaw could come from anywhere, and that quarantine did not help.

It was also known that air could contain its own type of no-see-ems. If you could get something hot enough...and make it airtight...then there was a good possibility it would be preserved against that invasion...until it was again exposed to the air. This was a huge step forward from the cave dwellers who burned cedar and pine, to later cultures who captured their product in airtight glass or metal so the air no-see-ems had no oxygen contact.

Then disinfectants were born. Liquid and otherwise. If you were infected, then you must be DIS-infected to get well. If your own body couldn't do it, then you needed outside help.

The color "white" became a signal of "cleanliness" because a lot of the dirt would show up on the surfaces, and if the whiteness was treated with disinfectants, you had it licked! Simple, it seemed, but Florence Nightingale spent her life trying to convince her fellow human beings of that simple fact with limited success.

She insisted that a germ-filled scalpel efficiently inserted would thrust its attached no-see-ems deeper into the wound, and also could carry them on to the next victim of operation. Historians suggest that, in the Crimean War, more soldiers were lost from infections than wounds...and time has born that out.

In the rapidly settled central parts of America, some information was slow in catching up, but to them, the word "hospital" meant "help" to just about everyone.

So it was that Miss Rowenna Moffat, as well as Miss Dollie Duffy and others, came on the scene in interesting times. They had the advantage of others before them because of those who could furnish "compacted" nuggets of information...called schools. Their individual reasons for attending the school were about as varied as their names, and the Girl with the Gun was among them. Her skill and training with the metal weapon was no match against the no-see-ems, but here she was, stepping into another battle.

The success of this battle would have to be the workings of her angel along with the promise that, though a person thought he was in charge of his steps, it was the Lord who directed.* Not only that, the direction of those steps was watched and numbered.** At times she recognized the presence of help and other times she was frightened spitless of what was ahead, but couldn't seem to find a reason to turn back.

These young women who were inspired by necessity along with Florence Nightingale, and were gathered together by Clara Barton and her organizational ability, the battle of the no-see-ems continued on a higher plane.

On the first weekend that Rowenna was not released to go home, Granddad hitched his yellow horse, Mustard, to his single seated buggy and climbed to the Ridge Road. Mustard, glad for any attention, tripped along the ridge and down into the hollow of Eureka Springs to the school. Granddad brought an offering of peanut/pecan brittle from the great aunts and greetings from her parents.

He was able to take her to a diner for a short visit... with emphasis on the "short." The hospital officials wanted it understood that she, and her time, belonged to them. Granddad took whatever time he could get.

It was with bittersweet acceptance that he listened to her relate how much she loved the hardest work she had ever done, and that she was so, so happy. She knew she was there with the help of her angel, and Granddad could not fault her for that, as he had been the one to teach her.

Mustard, not exactly happy to leave his favorite rider and pull Granddad home, could not have realized that he pulled a buggy containing a human who felt even worse than he did. It was a hard time for Granddad.

Rowenna returned to the huge white building with a feeling of returning home. She and Dollie found a secluded place and shared all of the candy...crunching and giggling like a couple of six-year-olds. There was not enough candy to pass around anyway...was there?

Then they carried the buckets of cooking scraps to the hogs out by the hospital's livery stable. They gathered the clean uniforms from the clothesline and brought them in. Ironing them would be tomorrow's job.

Along with the ironing of the uniforms, the bandage material, having been boiled in disinfectant, would be smoothed under the steaming surface of the sadiron as well. The heat of the iron created a totally sanitary bandage to be used again.

And so the battle of the no-see-ems was fought on yet another battlefield.

*Proverbs 16:9 and Psalm 37:23

**Job 14:16 and Job 31: 4 and 37

1916 AGAIN

Rowenna had purposely not been released from hospital duties to go home that first weekend. This stemmed from the idea that it was not good to let the girls think a weekend off was a deserved right, instead of a rare privilege.

Dottie was also held over...but she could not have gone home, anyway. Cedar Bluff was just too far away to be practical, especially in the winter.

There was another reason, actually more pertinent. Accidents could not be scheduled for the weekdays only...babies came when babies came...and humans broke their bones on almost any day on the week. Nurses, in their chosen profession, were expected to be in place when the accident occurred.

For instance, Black Rock Fish Camp was located north of the city and across the river. It was composed of a few scattered houses whose owners made their living by furnishing fish...fresh and dried and smoked...to the nearby settlements.

Black Rock River, so named from outcrops of coal, ran through the settlement and several young families managed an existence there. It was morning, now, and fisherman Papa Owens was finishing the milking. When he came in, then the family could eat.

The oatmeal had bubbled itself done and had been set aside to wait. The biscuits were browning in the oven, and five-year-old Elsie was positively perishing from hunger. Little sister, two-year-old Lucy, was hungry as well.

Mama Owens had been putting breakfast on the table when the baby woke up with a scream for attention. The tiny girl was very impatient when her diaper was uncomfortable...also, she could use a little food, if you please.

Small Elsie, at age five, was being taught to help by doing this or that easy chore, and she looked around, importantly, hoping for something she could do to advance the coming of food. That would be helping Mama, wouldn't it?

Lucy, almost three, was pulling insistently on Elsie's dress, hoping to encourage her in whatever she was deciding.

Now, Elsie knew not to stand on the three-legged stool. It was only to be used as a table to set her play dishes on, and not for stepping on to reach something. The stool was tippy, and she had already fallen a couple of times. This time, however, she would be extra careful, and it was a way she could help Mama. So that was all right…wasn't it?

Bringing the stool, she placed it in front of the stove. Finding a hotpot holder, she was ready…so she stepped carefully onto the stool. The handle of the oatmeal kettle was easy to reach, so she put the hotpot holder on the handle and pulled it nearer the edge. Carefully locking both hands on the handle, which was not hot at all, she lifted the pot and picked up one foot to step down.

Lucy was watching, and she knew the oatmeal kettle when she saw it. So now it was her turn to help. Reaching out, she clutched a handful of her sister's skirt tail and gave it a small tug which was certain to be a help…wasn't it?

By stepping one foot down, Elsie's remaining foot was on the edge of the stool and the little wooden stool did what it did best. It tipped, leaving Elsie to catch her balance and holding the oatmeal was just a bit more than she could handle.

Just as Papa stepped through the door with the milk, the stool went scooting and the very warm oatmeal went sliding over the lip of the pan onto a very surprised and indignant Lucy. The hot cereal flowed down one side of her head, over her shoulder and down her arm to the elbow. The loose night shirt she wore was immediately soaked with the clinging cereal and plastered hotly against her back.

Mama had just picked up the baby, and she rushed toward the screaming Lucy. Quickly sizing up the problem, she thrust the baby into Papa's hands, yanked a sheet from the bed, wrapped her daughter...cereal and all...and ordered Papa to take her to the hospital.

Papa put the baby on the floor and dashed through the door. Jamming the bridle onto old Buster, Papa leaped on... barebacked...and headed for the kitchen door. Scooping up the red-faced and screaming Lucy from her mother's arms, he thundered toward the town of Eureka Springs.

Buster may have been old, but he knew "fast" when he felt heels digging into his flanks. Twenty minutes later he thundered across the walking bridge and up the stone streets. Everyone knew where the hospital was, and a half an hour after Elsie stepped on the stool, Lucy was thrust into the arms of a young, white-uniformed lady.

At Papa's insistence, old Buster dashed to the stable at the back of the hospital and his rider leaped down and headed back toward the white building.

Miss Hollister had received the sheet wrapped bundle and sensed what it was. Not waiting for the elevator, she dashed up the stairs, two steps at a time and she pushed into the room with Nurse Bennett.

The nurse had a pulley attached to the splinted leg of a man in overalls, one leg of the pants split to reach the location of the break. Two students were helping to position the bone ends.

Rowenna was in the delivery room with Midwife Gardner holding the thrashing arms of a screaming young person at least a year younger than herself. She was supposed to be trying to quiet the girl, and also get an accurate pulse rate. Due to the thrashing, she had to keep starting over.

The midwife was scurrying around for this or that, knowing the girl could never deliver the six-month fetus that definitely had no heartbeat. Rowenna was intensely interested to see what was going to be done.

Nurse Bennett looked at the wrapped bundle and asked, "Burn...?" Miss Hollister nodded, still holding Lucy.

The experienced nurse accessed the problem and loudly yelled, "I need Moffat!"

Rowenna heard, and looked quickly at the midwife who ordered, "Go!" Rowenna went! Dropping the thrashing arm, she dashed next door to Nurse Bennett with a question in her eyes.

"MOFFAT...you know burns...? I can't leave here just now. Start cleaning. Willow tea in cabinet. Raw honey. Do what you can. Hollister, find me Duffy and get her here."

"Duffy...?"

"Blue cap. Kitchen I think. Hurry."

Rowenna took the oatmeal-smelling, dampish bundle from the receptionist, and put it on a gurney. The small girl was hoarse from screaming, and now groaned and snuffed. Peeling back the sheet, Rowenna was met with a smear of sticky cereal plastering her nightdress to her sides.

Nurse Bennett glanced and ordered, "Cut off clothes. You studied burns so do what you learned."

Biting her lower lip to stop the trembling, Rowenna took the scissors from the nearby drawer and snipped. Dollie stepped through the door, looking around, surprised. Nurse Bennett sternly demanded, "Duffy, do what Moffat asks and hurry. Start with bringing a basin of water and a cloth. Get with it!"

Dollie was fast, and the basin of warm water appeared. Rowenna soaked away by most of the cereal trying to ignore the screams by hurrying. To Dollie, "Will you get the willow water, another cloth and a big towel to put under her?" The cereal seemed to be about gone and the bowl of water appeared. Aspirins were available, but the willow was also good for pain, and it was liquid and ready.

With gentle fingertips, she smoothed the liquid onto the scarlet skin. The burns were warm to her fingers. She knew from her books that she should apply the moisture by fingertips to achieve better control and assess the depth of the burn by the skin temperature. She wished she knew more about the heat, and about what was "more...or less"...for comparison.

Dollie tipped up the edge of the towel to allow Rowenna to reach the tiny girl's back. Lucy was down to snubs and hiccoughs, but likely because she had worn herself out.

It was time for the honey. "Would you bring the honey, a small bowl and the paper squares." And added, "...and get small bandages."

Still with her fingers, she applied the strained, raw honey to the reddened skin and pressed the 4-inch squares of paper onto the honey to hold it to the skin and avoid moisture loss. The loss of moisture caused the scars to be more pronounced, the book had told her. A time or two Nurse Bennett stepped over to the bed and Dollie looked up with a question, but the nurse made no comment.

The little girl's eyes were drooping as the two blue caps gently wrapped the soft, sterilized bandages snuggly over the plastered paper squares. A man in work clothes appeared in the doorway. The nurse stepped over to speak to him, telling him his little girl was in good hands and had been treated. It was necessary that the wrappings not be moved for at least twenty-four hours, maybe more, to avoid infection, moisture loss and additional discomfort. She would be put to bed upstairs, and he would be permitted to see her but preferable not let her see him. She was exhausted and needed to rest.

It would be best they wait until tomorrow to visit her...did he understand? She assured him that he did right to get her here without trying to clean off the cereal. These nurses knew exactly how it was best done.

Rowenna and Dollie heard the word "nurses" and shot a glance at each other. Nurses! They were nurses! Of course they weren't, yet, but they loved the sound. The baby's papa walked away, taking the advice of not waiting to see her.

Nurse Bennett again. "Duffy...go upstairs and prepare a crib. We'll be up in a few minutes." And, with a nod, Dollie was gone.

The nurse's gruff voice startled Rowenna. "Good job, Moffat. This is what it's like to be a nurse. Everything happens at the same time. Now, this little girl is your patient at least today and tomorrow. Duffy will help and ask me anything you don't know. They tell me you passed your course with good grades, so we'll see how well you do."

Rowenna drew in a deep breath and words failed her, all except, "Oh, thank you. Thank you." Gathering the three-year-old in her arms, she headed for the stairs to the ward. One of the two cribs was moved into position and its white sheet and pillow put in place. The nurse removed the pillow and spread a small square of rubber.

"We're bound to have a wet bed, and we never use a pillow for a young child unless we are RIGHT THERE BESIDE THEM! It is too easy for young ones in pain to smother themselves."

Two blue caps nodded eagerly, and Rowenna eased the little girl down on the bed. A small sniff and a whine, and she seemed to drift into sleep.

"She may wake up hungry. Try a cracker, and later milk. Then potatoes. She should not be nauseous but best to be careful. All right, Moffat and Duffy, she's yours." And the nurse was gone.

In a matter of minutes, Scheduler Osborn hauled Dollie away to the galley. Potatoes to be peeled…no doubt.

Her patient being calmly asleep, Rowena edged away and hesitated at the door to the birthing room. The restless and flailing arms of the young woman were resting comfortably on the covering sheet, and the young face was in repose. Asleep? And there beside her sat a very young, very handsome man watching her sleep.

The midwife signaled with the wave of a determined chin for Rowenna to follow. In a closet stood a shiny metal bucket with a lid. "Moffat, I want you to take this bucket to the back fence. Do not empty in the privy. You'll see a shovel leaning against the back of the woodshed. Dig a hole about the size of this bucket and empty the contents. Do not look inside the bag. Cover it over smoothly and wash the bucket at the pump." Inviting no questions, the midwife turned away and busied herself with her instruments

Rowenna picked up the bucket and walked down the stairs. *Hmmm*…wonder what was in…NO! It couldn't be…but of course it was. She picked up the shovel and walked about two hundred feet to the back fence of the hospital property...out behind the livery and the hog pens. The loose soil shoveled easily and she lifted the lid of the bucket. A sodden cloth bag was there, about the size of a shoe box for a young child's shoes.

She tipped the bucket and slid the contents into the hole, returning the dirt and leveling the surface. There was something about this errand that was special and a bit sinister.

She returned the clean, dried bucket to the closet and turned to the midwife. Taking a deep breath for courage, she whispered, "Was...that the...?"

The midwife nodded and her gruff voice was low with emotion. "Yes, and I especially wanted you to do that chore. Generally I do it myself, but if you are going to be what I think you want to be, that is something you should know. Usually there are sweet babies to hand to the mothers but other times there are the...well, you know, now."

"But...is there no way to....?"

"No. We are not in charge. The decision was over when the girl stepped through our door. We helped in the only way we could, and by this time next year, she could possibly be a happy mother. If she had not come to us, she would be in the graveyard, instead."

"Oh...I just...I thank you for telling me." She turned and walked back to the crib and the peacefully sleeping Lucy. Such a darling. Her small chest rose and fell under the white bandages. What would be under those bandages...? Maybe she'd know tomorrow. Would she be just one big terrible scar? But her face... not a sign of the burn there but her ear had been brilliant red. It had been awkward to bandage the ear with her twisting and squirming, but Dollie was wonderful help.

She looked down into the crib and felt her eyes filling with tears. One baby gone forever...this one alive and healthy...a young woman alive, to yet be a mother. This hospital! What a wonderful place to be! Mopping her sleeve across her wet eyes, she looked up.

Angel, how did you work all of this out for me? Was it your idea...or did your Boss tell you what to do? If He gave you charge over me...then.... She ran out of words. The future was too scary, and maybe she didn't want to know just yet.

It was late and Dollie slipped in beside her. "Rowenna, you have to tell me about what we just did. How did you know what to do and how to do it? Nurse Bennett didn't say anything about how to...."

Rowenna thought that had been taken care of, but maybe not. "Well, it was...you see, I am the thirteenth kid of my parents and my ma learned a lot of things with the others." Certainly the truth, so far. So she added, "But I have a book that tells about a lot of things like this. It has pictures so there was no way not to know...and it explained that honey was totally pure and none of the no-see-ems can live in it. If we didn't have honey, we could have used grease."

"Oh, I just wondered. I'd like to have seen the book."

"You will see it next year in class. I think."

Dollie slipped out and climbed to the attic, still with a lot to a think about.

Little Lucy began to arouse. Rowenna had been eying the little potty chair, wondering if it would be familiar to Lucy. No way to know until she tried, but if it worked....

Quietly letting down the side of the crib, she reached for the small hands and pulled her to a sitting position. Lucy blinked at the soft lamp light, and then at Rowenna...with grave concern. Rowenna began to hum, "Jesus loves me, this I know. For the Bible..." Maybe the tune would be familiar to her...and it seemed to be.

Sliding the little girl to the edge of the bed, she eased her down to the floor. There were no burns on her feet. She stood on the rug while Rowenna moved the pink painted chair closer. Lucy eyed it from several angles, and it seemed all right.

"Let me help you," Rowenna said, softly, as she adjusted her gown and set her down. Once more she thought it would have been easier now, if she had been around small children. That

35

thirteenth kid thing, again. But she seemed to be picking up on the right things. Lucy stood and turned to look into the hole in the chair. She giggled and reached down for her panties but flinched when she moved her right arm.

"Wait! Let me help." Seeing the rocker nearby, she carefully lifted the girl and moved to the rocker. Lucy snuggled herself against Rowenna as they moved back and forth. Obviously, Lucy was accustomed to being rocked and hummed to. Too soon she was asleep, and Rowenna returned her to the crib.

Back in the rocker Rowenna drew her knees under her skirt and cuddled into the comfortable chair. She should go to bed, she knew, but maybe not for a minute. The book had instructed nurses on the need for conserving strength, but maybe just this once...?

Lucy's whimper woke her at two o'clock and a sip of water put her patient back to sleep. Rowenna thought of the nights she spent watching her sister with the measles...and little Nancy Parnell who also had a few bad nights.

Nurse Bennett woke her. "Good work, Moffat, but don't let it happen again. Sleep when you can. After she eats, we'll look under the wrapping and see how things are. We may need to wait until evening to change them." And she was gone.

MEANWHILE IN DOVER, ENGLAND

While Rowenna was by the gurney treating the burns of small Lucy, Granddad Hopkins was searching the newspapers from the larger cities of the Midwest for information. There was that thing called a dirigible that was a dream (nightmare?) of the German air force.

True, they had managed to design that mammoth balloon to cross the channel and drop explosive on British soil, but no major damage had yet been done. The sausage-shaped air ships took money and time and the skill of engineers, but they had no future as they were essentially un-controllable. Wind and storms and even barometric air pressure affected them. It was obvious to the old retired minister, Irvin Hopkins, that it was a waste and the Germans should keep at it, but not the English. But the Germans didn't they moved on to a more profitable venture.

Granddad signed. The brains, time and energy of the people on the islands should be used in a better way. Occasionally he picked up a snippet of information but it was mostly of a tiny winged aircraft that did not perform as hoped. There were the models, SA-1 and the SA-2, that had been set aside. A larger, more efficient engine was being tested. To decrease weight, the top wing of the biplanes was removed, and also the stabilizing platform to assist in landing would have to go. The wings were re-shaped for more lift, and the position of the rear wheel was moved to create a triangular landing.

The sons of rich men, who were so enamored with their toys, were not permitted even to test-fly them. Their skill was more profitably used in design and production. There were strong sons of farmers who slid into the seats of the hastily put together contraptions and fearlessly pointed them toward the skies. There were sons of native America who could "put on" a plane much like a suit of clothing and move into the clouds at one with the machine.

When the first plane lifted off the chalk cliffs of Dover, England, and soared across the channel to peer down on the battle waged in Belgium, the nation gave a cheer. The designers did not rest on their laurels, however, as it was certain that the German engineers (certainly no dummies themselves) were right on their rear ready to surpass them.

The Germans came up with the wonderful mechanism that shot a bullet through the propeller without hitting it. The gears of the engine and the weapon were designed to work together. Amazing! It took the English designers several months to copy the design, though by that time they were using, with remarkable success, an adaptation of the SA-3 aircraft that had the propeller on the back of the plane. That left the forward direction open for shooting.

But by then the wonderful German Albatross had taken to the skies. That winged, metal bird could carry bombs to be dropped rather than guns to be aimed. It had a longer period in the air and could carry a greater weight. So the English went back to the drawing board.

The SA-3 was a good observation plane. It could carry two passengers...a pilot and an observer. The observer would peer down to the battlefield with a telescope...determine where the greatest danger was amassing...sketching the position in relation to rivers and woodlands. This had to be done from varying heights from a moving and bumpy seat. It resulted in a bit of guesswork. It had to get better.

Observation was totally necessary and a great help, especially when a Morse Code was arranged to notify the actual troops on the ground in real time, but still these were more defensive measures rather than offensive, and it took offence to win a war. So the ground crew bent over their designs adjusting here and there, while the German Albatross was picking off strategic sites to drop off their explosives.

England, however, was turning out their SA-3 and a couple of other semi-effective designs at the rate of one new plane every hour.

THE REST OF DECEMBER

Rowenna and Dollie stood by with anxious eyes as Nurse Bennett peeled back the bandage on Lucy's arm. The skin was red and a bit puffy and it appeared very tender. Nurse Bennett nodded and appeared pleased.

"Moffat...Duffy...look closely. We see reddened skin which shows it is still alive. Fortunately, the cereal must have had a moment to cool before it landed on her. Also, she was brought within the first hour. She may have a scar for several years, but it will eventually fade. Clean carefully because skin is very tender. Then oil lightly and return the paper patches. Bind as you did before. Good job." And she was gone.

Dollie poured water from the sterilized jar and brought soft cloths. The small girl was amazingly patient, just seeming interested at what was going on and enjoying the attention from these grown-ups.

Then Lucy poked her finger in her mouth causing a drool. Hungry. Rowenna knew that much. Did she have the right to give orders…? "Uh…Dollie…could you go to the galley and see if there are potatoes and gravy? And milk…?"

"Sure," and she was gone, back in minutes with the potatoes, along with a spoon full of scrambled egg and a taste of applesauce. Lucy brightened at the sight of food and reached for the spoon. Dollie grinned with pleasure, and she held the plate while the little girl expertly transferred the food to her mouth.

Raising the side of the crib, Rowenna picked up the basket of sterilized toys. Blocks, dolls, wagons, wooden chains and a variety of wooden shapes that were colored with food coloring into soft shades. Lucy knew what to do with toys.

Dollie looked at Rowenna with a puzzled face. "Are all little girls this nice? I thought they would be yellin' on account'a hurtin'."

Rowenna shook her head. "I don't know. I'm the thirteenth and the youngest of all the cousins. But I think probably not." And Rowenna had no idea how right she was, but she would find out.

As the weeks passed, Rowenna never knew when she would be "held over" the weekend but that did not keep Granddad from making the trip up to the Ridge Road and down to Eureka Springs. At least he got to take her away from the school for a while and listen as she flooded him with the wonders of her new world and how much she was learning.

It was the last week of November when she was allowed to leave on Friday but must return Sunday afternoon. A whole day and a half. She hugged Ma and Pa and sniffed the kettles for what would be served for supper. Fried sweet potatoes with bacon, canned corn cut from the cob at its freshest. She knew the food choices were with her in mind when she saw the teacup-sized cornbread cakes just taken from the warming oven.

Home. It had been over a month since she had gone into her room. She pushed the door open and stepped inside. There was a strange degree of familiarity as though the room belonged to another person...perhaps a friend she knew well. The curtains... the pictures on the wall...the braided rug beside the bed...they all belonged to someone else.

This room had striped wallpaper instead of white painted walls. It had a left-over aroma of her dried flower bouquet instead of a faint smell of lye soap and disinfectant. She opened her closet door and looked at the clothes. They could have been for a girl of some other country. She looked at the wall shelf where she kept her schoolbooks, and the sight of the pink cover of one of them brought up the memory of darling little Lucy...who would eventually outgrow her scars.

A feeling of loneliness formed around her like a sudden fog that flows down the valleys in a temperature change. Lonely for what? She was at home...or was she? The hospital could get along without her. She felt herself swallow hard and sniff sharply, and the tiny sound seemed to echo in the silent room. She gouged her knuckles into her eyes refusing to let tears flow. Ma and Pa must not see this. She must pretend for a few hours that she was the same girl who had left almost three months ago.

She must learn to be two persons. That was something she had never considered. Tomorrow she must also remember that when she visited the aunts. They would be pleased, though, when she asked them for the white holster they had made to wear under her skirt. She had determined that the gun would go back with her and she would be very careful that Mrs. Cameron did not see it.

Even being called "Rowenna" instead of "Moffat" had a strangeness to it. As she walked down to the town of Wishbone on Saturday, she noted each familiar stone or bush with the memory of that other person. A very important part of her was clearly not here, but the aunts seemingly didn't notice.

She was hugged and humored and every word she said was hung onto and marked for future discussion when she was not there. Rowenna picked her words carefully. The aunts did not know that the person she knew they saw, really was not who she appeared to be. They would not care to hear about that other girl. Certainly they did not need to hear about the bucket she carried to the woods, and the tears she had shed as she had leaned against the woodshed.

They did, however, love to give her the little holster that just fit her 22mm Winchester. That...after all...was what had saved her life. They understood that. And they had chinky pin/pecan brittle for her and her friend.

And it was Sunday.

The church also belonged to that other girl. Even Wally was gone. He had made arrangements to attend the school in Fayetteville that the preacher had attended. She smiled as she looked at the church yard marquee. 'What on earth are you doing, for heaven's sake?"

There it was, and none of the shapes were put on by herself or cousin Wally. That just proved that no matter who she left behind, (that other girl she almost remembered?) life would go on. The marquee sign was completed without either of them. She obviously had no effect on the town. Left no vacancy when she departed. Like the hand removed from water, and the water immediately closed ranks as though the hand was never there.

She also had a wave of loneliness that Wally was gone, and apparently had a life without her...as she now had without him in Eureka Springs. But she'd see him at Christmas. She thought.

She was almost ashamed that she was so ready to return to the hospital. She must seem to be having a pang at leaving her family...and maybe she was...but it was overpowered by what was ahead. About what had happened yesterday and what had Dollie done that she was not a part of.

It was near the end of the year and she would get to see the new class of 1917. A few of the girls were already on board. The hospital actually encouraged those who could, to come as blue caps during December. It seemed to give them a better start to be sent home for Christmas and come back in January ready to learn.

For instance:

From the nearby town of Clifty, just a short way down Highway 23, there was Katie and Rosella, friends and schoolmates. They had long known what they wanted to do, and when they learned what they needed to know they would open their own place of business. Their Pa's would help. They would both be twenty years old sometime in the spring, and they had saved the money for a whole term for both of them. A flat one hundred dollars...and a year of their life would be spent in Eureka Springs.

Doris Lee was a local. She thought she might have a permanent job at the hospital, and she could be right. After all it took a lot of people to operate it.

There was Thelma. She had married at fourteen and was a widow at sixteen when her husband was killed in a farming accident. She had gone back home, but it was not the same. She needed something that was just hers and did not depend on someone else. Nursing seemed to fit.

Evelyn was from the community of Sourwood Valley. She had a waiting job of being nurse/receptionist to a doctor who lived in the valley. The Sourwood Valley was a beautiful piece of Arkansas land, and was fast filling with residents. She would be needed, and she was eager to get started with the classes for fear the doctor would hire someone else.

Marsha was totally tired of farm work. She had a dream, one night, that she managed to find a job that earned enough money so she could hire a fellow to pick the peaches and apples and beans and corn in her place. And dig up the potatoes and turnips and beets. She had joyfully told her family at breakfast and they had enjoyed a good laugh with her. But then her brother had said, "Sis, you need to go over to the nursing school in Eureka. I'll help you pay your way just to get rid of you!"

More laughs. But sure enough, he did! Pa chipped in a little and she had her fifty dollars.

Flora was part of a large family and when she finished school, there just didn't seem anything that interested her to do. The family decided to pool recourses and send her to nursing school. The worse thing would be that she could give family advice on health using what she learned. She'd likely get married anyway and live nearby. It only made sense and it sounded good to Flora.

Cora came from the next county to the east. Came on the train from up at Echo Mountain.

She was a big girl, well-built and strong and a full five feet nine inches tall. Her ma had passed on leaving her on a lonely farm with a tight-wad father who thought food and a roof over her head was pay enough his daughter for her to keep house for him. Cora disagreed. She decided to pay herself, and thought her services were worth one dollar per week so when she washed his clothes, she extracted one dollar each week. She even decided she would like a Christmas gift from him and that was five dollars. And of course she should have had a birthday present each year of her life. She was seventeen, so that made seventeen dollars to catch Pa up to date with his duty.

She fixed a good supper for him and left him with a clean house and all of his clothes being freshly washed. She picked a moonlit night, slipped out and bridled Pa's least favorite horse and tossed on a well-worn saddle. She led the horse quietly away from the house and tied him.

When Pa went to sleep, she picked up the satchel of her few favorite belongings and met the horse in the woods. On horseback they moved along on the moonlit Ridge Road to the whistle stop of Briarwood Junction. She spent the night in a handy barn on a bed of hay. Near the Junction, she passed a young man carrying a huge pack on his back, so, as she related the story to the girls who would be her classmates, she had said to the fellow:

"'Friend, I got me a old horse here that needs a home. You interested in takin' 'im on?' And that fellow says to me he don't have no money and I sez to 'im, 'who asked for money? I'm a angel, I sez to 'im, and I've been sent to give you a present. Will you take it?' Then I walked away, wishin' I could fly to convince 'im I really was a angel."

She grinned a happy grin over the wonderful joke. "Then I told a story to myself about how he'd explain a gift from a angel to his family. I walked the last mile and caught the Frisco Mail Train, and here I am.

"Never did remember how I knew about this here school, the way Pa kept me tied down. Could be a angel put the thought in my head. Reckon that could'a been it?" And then she smiled her attractive smile.

Rowenna, like all the others, was fascinated with the story, and she was fairly certain it truly had been Cora's angel. She guessed that the young man sorely needed the horse and that was another action of an angel. Maybe his angel. She said nothing, as this was clearly Cora's story.

Then Cora added, soberly, "I never did figger how I got words about maybe havin' angels in my head tellin' me to do this or that."

Rowenna still said nothing, but certainly had thoughts. "Yeah, you and me, too," was her first thought.

Of course there was Dollie, but she had already told her story.

Next there was Lina. Her story came out in bits, likely because she couldn't bear to tell it all at once. She came with her mother and had spent at least an hour with Mrs. Cameron in her office.

It seemed that Lina's mother had been stolen away at age thirteen when she was on an errand for her ma. She had been walking down the road and a buggy stopped to offer a ride. She thanked him and refused. She'd been told to never accept rides from strangers.

The man stopped the buggy and chased her. He caught her, tied her hands together and forced her into the buggy. He took her a long way to a cabin on the side of a hill and it had the apparatus of a moonshine still in the back yard.

The girl was chained in a small shed and the door was locked. There was a pile of hay in the corner and she tried to sleep but couldn't for shaking with fear. The next day he took her to the kitchen and chained her to the wall with enough length to reach the stove and the cabinet.

She was supposed to cook his meals. He loosed her long enough do to other chores but always in his sight. He told her she'd never find her way out of the woods because he had twisted directions around when he came in. So she just as well make up her mind that she was here to stay.

She was even chained to the bed at night for two whole years. He thought by then she would not run away and he was right. She had no idea of where to go, and sometimes she wasn't sure there was even a world outside of the cabin.

At sixteen she had a baby boy and she was so pleased. She thought things would be better. Maybe they were, but she was still a prisoner. Two years later Lina was born. She did the best she could to teach the children to read from any scrap of paper that appeared anywhere.

When her son was fourteen, he ran off without even saying goodbye. She didn't blame him because his pa beat him almost daily. He just flat-out got tired of it and left. Two years later he sneaked back in the middle of the night, woke his ma, and made her come outside to talk.

"Ma, you gotta leave here. I'm gonna hop a train and go till they throw me off and then I'll hop another one. I'm never comin' back but I wanted to do this one thing for you for bein' good to me. They's a town about two days north'a here. You gotta slip out with Lina and walk with the mornin' sun on your right shoulder and the afternoon it'll be on your left. You get to town and there'll be someone to help.

"You listen to me, Ma, 'cause this is the onlyist thing I can do for you. You gotta get Lina away from Pa 'cause you know what Pa'll do with her, purty as she's gettin'. You promise me, Ma?" And he had taken her by the shoulders and squeezed with his strong hands to put emphasis on his words.

45

Before she could answer, he had disappeared into the trees, and she was left staring into the darkness at nothing. The hoot of an owl reminded her she'd better get back in the house before she was missed.

That year Lina was fourteen. Her ma had watched her as she worked and thought about what her son told her. Yes, they had to leave…but how?

She finally figured a way she thought would work. Using her slim knowledge of herbs, she gathered leaves from the datura plant with its pain killing properties. It was possible to die from its use, but she raked her memory for what she thought she knew. How much was it that put a person to sleep? But didn't kill him?

She could really think of no other way, so she baked a blackberry cobbler, his favorite, and treated his favorite corner piece with a liberal quantity of the mashed datura leaves. Sure enough he became sleepy and went to bed earlier than usual. With ropes, she tied his arms and legs to the four corners of the bed, and the chain that chained her in the shed was put around his neck and looped to the bedpost.

That was a daring move, because she really didn't need that chain to hold him but was determined to do it. He roused slightly, but then settled back in his drugged sleep. It was hardly dark when she and Lina picked up their clothing that had been stuffed in a pillowcase. They ran down the road for the first hour and reached the Ridge Road. Slowing to a walk, they prepared to hide if someone came along. No one did.

About daylight, they reached a farmhouse with a large barn. The man would be milking. Perfect. Giving the envelope to Lina she hid by the road and the girl took the prepared envelope to the door and knocked.

When a child answered the door, she handed him the envelope and said, "Give this to your daddy. My pa has a message for him. He said don't open it yourself." Then she turned, and when she was out of sight of the door, she ran.

It was mid-morning when the farmer read:

"Sir: Over to the still they is a man tied to a bed and can not move. Would you be so good and get the shrif to let him loose so he don't die? If you do that you will save two more lives. I thank you for this faver."

The man chuckled. "Feature that! Someone finally decided to do in the old moonshiner. Reckon I'll go do what the note asks. Not that he deserves it."

Mother and daughter hid in the woods and rested until noon, then headed straight ahead. They walked all day, avoiding traffic on the road, until they reached a church. A man was working in the yard, and her ma asked him, "Would you be the preacher?" He was.

She had carefully decided what to say.

"Preacher, would you be knowin' a place where a woman and a girl could work for their keep? We ran into hard times, but we're healthy and we can work hard…if you was to know of someone."

The preacher instantly thought of the old couple who would very much like to live in their house, but just weren't able to manage it without help. Lina and her ma spent the next four years there…around books and newspapers. First the old man died…then the woman.

On her deathbed, the woman gave Lina exactly $50.00 in her hand and told her to go on to Eureka Springs and find the nursing school. She was to tell them she had experience with sick, and she wanted to be a nurse.

Eighteen-year-old Lina and her mother showed up at the hospital at 10:00 on the second of December. Lina took over when her mother seemed too broken-up to continue.

"Miz Cameron, it was this way. After what we been through, we got the money for the school but we got no place to live. My ma is strong, and she thinks you might need someone for cookin', or somethin', or maybe garden work. She can do anything, but she needs a place to sleep. She got to thinkin' maybe you needed to keep a fire at night or somethin', and she could do that. She'd be glad for a bed in the kitchen or in a closet. She'd sleep anywhere and she'd work for food while I'm in school to be close to me and have a place to be."

Mrs. Cameron was certain they needed help. They always needed help, and if all she needed was a bed…?

Lina continued, "Miz Cameron, my ma don't hardly know about people. She wasn't let to see no body for all her life, but she was bound and determined to see it didn't happen to me. If you could…maybe…?"

The supervisor turned toward the girl. "Lina, I know you are going to be a wonderful nurse, and your mother has a job for the whole year and maybe even longer if she wants it. Come with me while I take her to the Galley and get her started. I want you to know where she is, then we'll get you set up."

So Lina smiled at the other "blue caps" as she proudly adjusted her own cap on her head full of red curls. "I just can't hardly think I'm gonna be a real nurse. It just seems like a gift from someone I don't know who must'a knowd the inside'a me and wanted to help."

Rowenna could keep still no longer. "Lina, think about your angel? This help is something an angel might give, don't you think?"

This conversation had been after Granddad had delivered her, along with two bushel baskets of beautiful red Ben Davis apples from the Moffat orchard to the hospital. It was not unusual for the hospital to receive a gift of food…but two whole bushels of Ben Davis apples…!

Every girl could choose one to eat raw, and there would still be apple crisp for breakfast and apples fried with sweet potatoes for supper the next day. Something as wonderful as these must be used right up not be let to run the risk of spoilage.

Rowena would next go home on Christmas. She was scheduled for December 19 to January 5, but that, of course, could change. She would see Wally and she might even see Nathan. She'd thought about him on so many occasions and how helpful he was when she was trying to make up her mind. She wondered now whether he had managed to get what he wanted.

THE AMERICAN RED CROSS

While Rowenna's Granddad was searching the newspapers for information that he hoped he wouldn't find, a lot of other things were going on.

In August 1914, England had joined with France to declare war on Germany. They hardly had a choice...Emperor Kaiser Wilhelm's 'great rush to the sea' had actually been successful. Belgium had fallen to Germany and their army was now nibbling at the edges of France.

England did not go to the war...it was brought to them.

Where there was war, there was blood. Where there was blood, there should be someone to tie on a bandage and sop up the loss. Basic premise. Where were the doctors and nurses who should be along with the wounds and the bleeding? In America... that's where.

Actually, there was that thing that Clara Barton had worked for...the American Red Cross. The organization was actually founded in Switzerland with the help of Israel in 1876 but was rapidly picked up by America.

While the military was thinking of machinery and explosives, the Red Cross was gathering supplies and medicine and recruiting trained help. There were volunteers aplenty... for the necessary duties of laundry and cooking. But more was needed.

Many wealthy persons and companies made donations of money and blankets, food and medicine. Old Granddad was impressed...Americans were such generous, caring persons. He would like to have been able to send them millions if he just had millions to send.

Little did he know he would send them something far more valuable to him than money.

In l914, England began accepting volunteers and there was no lack. Besides the adventurers, there were those who knew they were fighting for their very own freedom...for the lives of their families and themselves.

The military needed men who could shoot and man the gun emplacements and fight from the trenches, and the needed strong girls to replace the men on the home front. English doctors of all kinds joined along with the other skilled persons and were put in the trenches along with the farmer's sons who could actually carry the baggage and shoot with accuracy.

Result: Doctors died in the trenches and so did the soldiers they could have possibly saved. The American Red Cross saw this happening and began to search for secondary medical personnel... not specialized surgeons, but trainable persons with skills in that direction. Where would they find them...? Well, there were the nursing schools and the pharmacy schools, and there were barber colleges that taught a smidgeon of life-saving methods.

All along with the ship loads of all-wool blankets, there went bleached cotton for bandages and crates of iodine. The Red Cross called for American sheep growers and cotton farmers to strive for much greater production.

And they also needed warm bodies. There were country girls who were strong...and immigrants who could speak and understand English fairly well, and there were girls from the American Midwest who were accustomed to hard work. The girls answered the call in droves. Amazing, actually.

They also needed men. Men who were patriotic and strong, who could dig trenches, follow orders and shoot straight. The men of the new country of America lined up to volunteer. Anyone could see that they would eventually be drafted, so they'd just go and get it over with.

These persons would make up the strength of the American Red Cross where there was an abundance of forethought...so much more so than the actual military had managed. Granddad Hopkins of Wishbone, Arkansas, read what he could find about these extraordinary persons. Even the name intrigued him. Red...? And Cross...?

With the knowledge acquired from his ministry, he remembered the time a scarlet (red) cord was hung from a window and many lives were saved.* And later God's son was clothed in scarlet (red) and he was crucified (on a cross) and many hearts and souls were saved.**

Could there be any connection...surely not, but it did give one pause to consider. At any rate, the American Red Cross seemed to have extraordinary success and time was of the essence.

Before the battle crossed the channel and entered England, the volunteers from America were on site. Loaded hospital ships, and those whose aim behind the guns would fight off the attacks of the deadly German U-boats...all came to help.

Cleanliness first, whenever possible. Strong arms that could bring the wounded to the ship to be treated and out of danger... but oh!...how they needed medics! Strong young men with a specialized knowledge. Battlefield medics were needed. They simply must be found.

Not a white coated doctor with a scalpel, but a strong body with a clever brain and a skillful hand. Not a spotless room. They needed someone to carry or drag the filthy and bloody wounded back to safety and it should NOT be a fellow soldier who must stay in the fight, pushing forward.

Hence the roots of the Red Cross' intensive sixteen week course sprouted to life. Somehow they must find those persons prepared for the horrors of what they would have to do and the will to go do it. The plan was later improved and refined, but in 1916 there was no time for the finer points.

Wishbone, Arkansas had someone to offer.

Nathan Wilkinson had reached the age of twenty-one and was within sight of his dream, to be a certified pharmacist and set up business in his tiny hometown. It was all he wanted.

But Nathan also read the papers. He was of a certain intelligence and could clearly see that America would be called on to help Brother England now, or they would be fighting on

American soil eventually. A bully does not give up when he's winning, and that European country of Germany had been taken over by bullies.

Nathan's dream of being soon back in Wishbone began to fade as he saw that the courses he had finished in the last four months placed him in the center of those best suited to volunteer, and would possibly be first to be conscripted. The Red Cross was pleading for men just like Nathan. They were begging for Nathan, himself.

He knew on the first of December that his decision had been made, though he pretended had not been. He would go home for Christmas and make his decision. He would see his friends and he would see how "little Reena" was doing with her own dream. He pushed back the thought that perhaps his friendship with her had changed.

Along with pushing away what he knew was his future, he kept clinging to the idea that "Wally's little cousin" occupied a spot in his mind only because of the kidnapping incident when he had helped her. He would have felt the same way with any other girl from Wishbone...wouldn't he? Anyone who was almost five years younger than he. Wouldn't he...?

How old would she be now...as if he had not figured that up so many times. Let's see...5 years from 21 made 16. No, her birthday was just before Christmas. That meant she would be looking at 17. A year made a big difference in the way it sounded.

In letters, there were comments that she was still in Eureka Springs with her sister. He knew that was not true. Wherever she was, she was with herself. She might let Wally be there with her occasionally, and possibly Nathan himself if he had a little time to get better acquainted.

Maybe she was a "loner" as some said, but Nathan would better have described her as "self-contained." There was a big difference. For the self-contained, there was occasionally room for another person to be with them, but they did not depend on another person to help them to be complete. Come to think on it, her cousin Wally was a lot like that as well.

While Wally, on the other hand, paid no attention to the war. He was not great on studying, but when he had to, he did it with all his heart. He had finally given in and enrolled in the college in Fayetteville.

Not really a seminary, but it was where preacher Clemmons had gone and that seemed good enough for Wally. If God wanted him to do all this studying…and apparently he did…Wally might sigh with resignation but he would begin.

But, hey! It wasn't nearly as hard as he had expected. He had spent the last half a year conducting a Bible familiarity study at his church, and he had taught himself a lot…and maybe helped others as well. The study had not been in his plans, and neither was the college. He was happy stacking cans in Wilkinson's Market, but it seemed God had other ideas. Wally knew his Bible well enough to know that God always wins…sooner or later… and the young man didn't want a horse having to straighten him out like the story of old Balaam's donkey. ***

Wally had no time or thought for the war across the ocean. He had fought enough of a war in his own mind, and God had won. So now he was paying reparation…actually preparing himself to be a preacher, that is, if God insisted.

But Nathan knew his position was different. He wasn't sure just how, but he would know more after the Christmas break.

There was still a bloody scuffle on that little bump of land that jutted out into the English Channel. Strange name of Ypres (pronounced I-per). It was just like the French to put in letters that did not pronounce and leave out the ones that did. Like Dunkerque instead of Dunkirk.

Red Cross sixteen week course. January 15 to May 15. Then processing to be on board the ship by July 1. Nathan knew the schedule and had heard the pleas from the Red Cross. He had received the mailing…as did the barbers and hospital orderlies who were in training. But, of course, he had not yet made up his mind to go. Or so he tried to convince himself.

There was the promise that the compressed training would enable the students to pass the requirements for pharmacist, and the test would be offered if desired. Well, that was what he wanted…wasn't it? Sooner or later he would have to go and that was clear. But he had not made up his mind…he told himself over and over.

He would go home to his friends and family and his mind would be clearer. Maybe he would throw a hook and line in Little Mulberry River and pull out a catfish or two. One should not be in a hurry to make life-changing decisions. There would be time to ponder. Three whole weeks.

He should have written to Rowenna to see what her plans were, but how was that any of his business? He had talked himself out of writing several times, but now he wished had been braver and done it.

*Joshua. Chapter 2, verse 18 and Chapter 6, verses 22-23.
**Matthew. Chapter 27. Specifically verse 28
***Numbers 22: 20-31

CHRISTMAS 1916 AT WISHBONE, ARKANSAS

The month of December began well, with just the right amount of cold weather. There was the usual talk on the Spit and Whittle bench, on the days it was warm enough to be outside… and in the diner when it wasn't.

There was that war still going on…and what was your family planning for Christmas? Were the ones in Fayetteville and Bentonville going to be able to come home? No matter if you had lived in Fayetteville for twenty years, if you were born in Wishbone, then that was your home. Everyone knew that.

Granddad Hopkins said what he needed to say and thought a lot that he didn't say because no one wanted to hear it. They couldn't help anything just by hearing his worries, so why bother?

There was that American Red Cross organization pleading for volunteers and he would have applauded their efforts except for Rowenna…and lately, for Wally. Then he chided himself for his self-centeredness at being willing to send other men's children but not his own.

So now Wally, if he was farther along with his lessons, wouldn't they maybe defer him? No...they'd just be glad to get a "chaplain," according to what he read. Hopefully it would be someone who had an inkling about the afterlife and could perhaps give comfort to someone in immediate danger of going there. Would that be Wally? And to be honest, Granddad had to admit it was.

Wally might hesitate and try to turn away, but when headed in the right direction he was impossible to stop. And now he was over eighteen and clearly his own man and capable of making his own decisions. He needn't worry about Wally...but tell that to a grandpa.

And that girl. At least she was safe. A young nurse buried within the hills of Arkansas would be impossible to find... wouldn't she? But Granddad knew her well. She would be just as likely to wave a flag and yell "here I am" as she would be to hide.

And the thing was, she would not need to be trained...she already had the Gold Certificate. He sighed a long sigh as the morning talk went on around him, and him not hearing a word of it. Maybe he'd saddle up Mustard and take a trip up to the hill house. She wasn't there yet, but her ma and pa were. Also, that old horse was fair pining himself away, hanging his head over the gate and looking at the road.

And in hilltop house preparations were being made. The two sons who were woodcutters had brought four wagonloads of wood to keep the big house warm when the family all came in.

Some of the thirteen children could come early but had to leave for their jobs, and some would be later. Too bad, but Ma and Pa liked it better that way. If they all came at once, the noise would likely crack the walls wide open and no one would remember a word that was said....

Ma would be baking all sorts of goodies, and the daughters would bring their own. Such a lot of food...almost sinful, it seemed. Ma had already decided that what was left could be sent to Rowenna's hospital.

They'd already sent apples and both white and sweet potatoes. They'd sent cornmeal ground from their donkey-operated grinding mill. They'd even sent eggs until it got cold and the hens laid off production. With Old Irvin making his weekly trip, it was very handy to send things to the school.

The great aunts down on Main Street would stay open for the Christmas gift-buying days, but they made sure to stir up a batch of the chinky pin/pecan candy their little girl liked. Maybe she'd have so much fun at home that she'd give up that crazy idea of hers of being a nurse. One could hope.

Wally almost resented the holidays but only because it made him two weeks later with his certificates. This year and next year and then he'd see which way he should go.

One thing about this decision of Wally's to go back to school…his four much older sisters were so terribly proud of him, they sent gifts of goodies and occasionally a pair of socks. Maybe he'd get new shirts for Christmas and then he wouldn't have to wash so often. Being a student, things looked different.

Even student Dollie Duffy would get to go home. Her cousin would be bringing his wife to Wishbone for Christmas shopping and would pick her up. She'd get back somehow, though, because she would get a WHITE HAT in January and be a real student! The people in Cedar Bluff would be so proud! She'd miss the time with Rowenna, though.

Several of the blue caps chose to stay and that would help keep things running. The thing about a hospital, it didn't get a vacation. According to Nurse Bennett, people seemed to wait until the holidays to get sick…crack a bone…break out in some unexplainable rash…or have a baby.

But Rowenna would come home. She put on her "street dress" and waited. Granddad would be there, but he would want to take her to the diner first. She nodded approval. It had become an expected routine to have time when he could have her to himself for a few minutes, and she could face him with whatever had puzzled her…or maybe share something exciting that she'd done.

She couldn't however, tell him about the trip to the back fence with the bucket and shovel. That was just too sad and horrible but not as bad as if the girl had not had the hospital to come to. Granddad would not enjoy hearing about that.

He would have Mustard between the buggy shafts. The horse would whicker and toss his head to see her, and Granddad would have a carrot for her to give him. She missed that old yellow horse about as much as she missed anyone else...at least she thought about him that much. Maybe...just maybe...she'd get a chance to ride him this time. Of course she could not straddle his back like she used to, and riding side-saddle cramped her knee. Sometimes growing up was a bit of a pain, especially if one must wear a long skirt.

She waited by the gate and here he came...Mustard tossing his head and excitedly jingling his harness rings.

The guard at the gate smiled and waved. She liked that fellow...standing there for hours at a time to keep the hospital safe. He wore his gun openly in his holster so everyone would know. It had to be a positively boring job.

A half an hour later the old horse was trotting along the brick-paved street toward the climb that would take them to the Ridge Road.

She left the horse and buggy at Granddad's. She insisted on climbing to the hilltop house on foot on the worn path. Almost a quarter of a mile and almost straight up. She'd always liked that path, and every stone and flowering bush had seemed like a friend at times.

But this time it was different. When she stepped from the buggy, she was in another life...one she used to know, but now seemed more strange than familiar. It was like being in Laverne's plays when she pretended to be another person. Laverne was very good at that, but Rowena was not. She had feelings of uneasiness as though she had no business to be there.

Then Ma and Pa! So familiarly different. More wrinkles, and their wrinkles fitted them so well. She loved every one of them, just like she loved the wrinkles on Aunts Sophrenia, Georgiana and Cecelia. Ma looked at Rowenna with pleasure and satisfaction like she was admiring a perfect bed of petunias by the doorstep.

And Ma couldn't keep from touching her. A comforting arm lightly on her shoulder…a soft pat on her forearm. And Pa… patiently waiting his turn, a smile in his eyes as well as his mouth. So much love…and her the thirteenth kid. A body'd think they'd be wore down by now and completely out of love. They asked so little of her and were so happy with what they got. How could she be so fortunate?

She'd hang around the house until some of the others came before she went to town. She wanted to walk by the church… the BIG THREE diners…the Cryer Newspaper where her sister worked. She wanted to walk, all alone, to the pier and watch Little Mulberry River flow by.

Why did she want to do this? If she really admitted that she was just trying to retrieve a bit of her past, it might be scary but true. One must not let pieces of their life get away. Much of it belonged to that girl whose clothes were in the closet of the room that no longer seemed to be hers, but still, the mental pictures were important.

A lot of miles away in the state capitol city of Little Rock lists were being made. It was going to be necessary for the military to accept the aid of the American Red Cross to make up for preparations for war that they had neglected. Also, there was the need to replace the medical personal that Brother England had sent to the trenches in order to be "fair" and not "play favorites" with who was being sent to possible death.

An assignment was made to the various regions of America to search for those who might answer the call for medical help. The new nursing schools of the states, and there were quite a number, were assigned to list their students who had completed the requirement for nursing, heading the lists with the Gold Certificates students

Additionally, a list should be made of the young men who had even a smidgen of medical knowledge, and more important, were strong, apt and teachable. These could be gleaned from hospital orderlies, barbers and pharmacists. These persons were not to be notified yet, just their names were to be furnished. Important lists made.

This was to be accomplished immediately, so that the lists could be returned to the headquarters by the first of year 1917.

Rowenna went with Pa when he did the chores and when he went to cut the cedar limbs to burn in the fireplace because they made such a Christmassy smell. She clipped a bouquet of limbs with red berries for the table. She tried to convince herself that everything was normal.

She shelled chinky pins for the fruit cakes and made small talk with Ma. She whipped up the cream for the pumpkin pie she knew had been scheduled for lunch just for her. She told Ma a few of the experiences she thought Ma would like and all the time she felt herself oozing away from her Wishbone life. This was just a conversation with a wonderful lady the "other girl" knew. This lady appreciated the efforts of that other girl, but she did not know the new one. How could she...?

Rowenna's mind tried to hold to the past at least for these two weeks. Not very successful. WHAT was going on? Did this happen to others? What was Wally feeling now? It seemed a half a year since they had a real talk.

Ma said he would be here for Christmas dinner...but that was no time to talk. Really talk. She had a good feeling about Wally because he seemed to be doing so well in the summer... Ma thought.

She might not even have a chance to see Jewelee as she would also be busy with her own family. And then, seriously, what could they talk about after the first seven minutes? They had always been very different, and the glue that had held them together was the church and the school, the town and their ages.

The church, school and town were in the past. What was left was their ages and there were hundreds of other 17-year-olds with whom she also had nothing in common. How sad, actually.

Now, Dollie...that was another matter. She was eighteen but that didn't matter. They could chatter together for hours just like a couple of squirrels. WHAT was going on? Angel…? What is going on?

Then Ma said, "Oh, honey! I need to you to do an errand. If I make those custard pies for Shirley Ann tomorrow, I'll need nutmeg. You wouldn't mind…would you…?"

So she slipped on a heavy jacket…one that belonged to that other girl. She grinned to herself about how nice it was that she and the other girl were the same size. She swung along the path down to Wishbone enjoying the brisk breeze on her face.

She stepped through the door of the WM and breathed in the familiar smell. She looked up into the face of a strange young man who smiled as though he knew her. NATHAN! Not in overalls and shirt…or waist pants and jacket. He was wearing pleated pants, tucked in shirt and a tie. Eyes and mouth both open, she stared at him.

"Rowenna! I hoped you might be coming down. Saved me a trip up to your house and risk missing you. I hope you have a little time to talk."

He came right to the point. Rowenna considered. Ma didn't need the nutmeg until tomorrow so that meant she had time. Uh…hey…Ma didn't need nutmeg at all! She'd done it again? She knew I wanted to come to town so she sent me.

"I have time. Where do you want to go?"

"The diner…?" He took his jacket from the rack and followed her to the door, then walked beside her down the familiar sidewalk to the stores. Possum Creek rushed by the sidewalk, force-fed from Big Mouth Springs a quarter of a mile up toward the ridge. "How have you been?" There had to be a starting point and this was it.

A sigh and an effort to settle on one thought. "Well, I got to stay at the hospital but I still don't go to classes. But you know, Nathan, they treat me different and I have the strong feeling I will never be in class."

"Do you care?"

"No, because I get to help with a lot of things. Tell me about you. Do you like what you're learning?"

"I'm learning more than you can ever guess, and I'll tell you about it when we sit down."

The store windows were decorated with cedar, silver ribbons and tinkling bells. The doors sported wreaths of red berries. An aroma of cinnamon candy was everywhere.

Billowing steam of apple cider spiced with cinnamon arose from a kettle on a small stove. He ordered sugar cookies and cider and took them to the tiny table that made it so easy to talk.

He began, "I may have a change of plans. It seems I already have a valuable skill needed by the Red Cross in Europe and they want to give me a 4 month quick course and send me over there. How's that for saying everything in one sentence."

"Four months, huh." It wasn't a question.

He nodded without comment.

"Where in Europe?"

"Belgium…maybe. A tiny nation caught between Germany and the English Channel."

"What will you be doing?"

"I haven't agreed to do it, yet. It was only an invitation…a request, and a promise that it would qualify me as a pharmacist."

Rowenna nibbled her cookie and sipped the cider. Delicious and very festive. She looked up and met his eyes. She could now do for him what he had done for her. "Nathan, you've already made up your mind, and you know it. You just haven't admitted it to yourself. I know that because that was where I was when you decided for me to get on over to the hospital."

His turn to be silent and concentrate on the cider. Then, "You're seventeen now. Happy birthday."

"Yeah, well, I didn't have anything to do with it. It just got there on its own effort." A small grin, and then, "Nathan…? Do you ever feel like you might be two people and end up arguing with yourself, or wondering how your old self got left behind?"

A nod. "Off and on most of my life. But I think both of my selves are agreeing that I must do this. All of us fellows are thinking, actually knowing, that there'll be a draft in a year or so, and then we'll do what we're told. Now, I at least know where I would be going, and what I would be doing."

"What would that be?"

"Likely rescuing wounded from the battlefield and administering first aid. Or just trying to get them to the back of the line to be evacuated. I can only imagine what a war is like, but now the wounded are being tended by untrained fellow soldiers and that takes the helpers away from the battle. Doesn't seem to work well. How about you?"

"I really don't know. Wishbone thinks I'll maybe set up to work here, but there's no one to work with and I can't do it alone. And the thing is, I don't really…I mean, I can't see myself doin' that for a long time. Working in the hospital is very interesting and exciting, but maybe not forever."

A couple minutes of silence. "Pa bought that little house at the back of THIMBLES AND SPOOLS. Said it was for me and he'd rent it for me till I need it. I hate to disappoint him but I just don't know."

"Rowenna, you wouldn't believe the times I thought of you and of this little diner, wishing we were there. You're so easy to talk with."

Rowenna considered how she should put this. She felt like she knew him better than she actually did. "Times I thought of gettin' your address and seein' how you were. Then I remembered you were studying, and surely you'd be home Christmas. I hadn't thought much about the war, with things going on over in Eureka. I thought Granddad was doin' enough worryin' for the both of us. The thing is, though, he can't do anything about it. The war, I mean." A hesitation and a glance out the window. "But maybe you can."

He sighed and nodded. "One question. Do you really like what you're doing?"

After a moment. "I love what I do but I hate that it has to be done. The rest of my feeling is sorta caught in the middle. Does that make sense…?

"Perfect sense. If I accept the Red Cross..." but he was interrupted.

"Maybe you should say WHEN you accept...."

"I stand corrected. When I accept the invitation from the Red Cross, I will be gone from 15 January to 15 May without coming home. Then I will have a month to get things together before I have to go. I'll work out of a hospital ship until the British push Germany back from the point of Belgium that is closest to Britton. The mouth of the Somme River is also a military objective. That's absolutely all that was promised, except that a combat medic is often expected to work under fire. And that plans always change."

"Under fire...?"

"Live ammo overhead. You'd know better than any other girl what that's all about. Incidentally, do you still carry your 22mm?"

She grinned appreciatively. "Not yet. My aunts made me a cloth holster to wear under my skirts, and I'm taking it back with me. Sometimes I go see Laverne and Granddad doesn't want me on the streets unarmed."

Nathan took the hand that held the last cookie. "Believe me...I don't want that either! I need you around to help figure out my next step."

She playfully jerked away her hand. "Only if you'll help me unravel my own puzzles." Then she added with a chuckle, "The hospital supervisor knows about me, thanks to Jadeen, and says she doesn't ever want to see my gun on the premises. I'll be sure she doesn't see it."

It seemed time to go. They both knew this visit was just to break the ice and make certain they were still swimming in the same pond...so to speak. Also, it was a preliminary "goodbye." Several questions answered. A few more questions to go.

He opened the door for her to step down from the diner. Instinctively, he reached for her hand as any young man would do for a girl and did not release it as they started up Main Street toward the WM. Rowenna made no move to retrieve her hand. That told him a lot but there was still a long way to go.

At the WM he picked up the nutmeg and put it in her hand. She told him, "See you later," smiled and left. He watched her walk away. Seventeen. That sounded so much better than sixteen. She understood exactly what was said to her, and she did not seem frightened. Only concerned.

Nathan's Pa watched him watch her. He smiled a small smile of satisfaction. If anything could change the stubborn mind of his son, it could be this girl. He must not be allowed to do what he was surely planning to do.

While Rowenna and Nathan were in the diner, the Frisco Railway locomotive was chugging its way through the Arkansas hills toward Memphis and points east. Among the official mail pack was a request to the Memphis School of Nursing to furnish a list of their Gold Certificate graduate nurses, including all others who have Certificates of Completion.

The schools were requested to furnish any personal notations they wished, as most of these young ladies would be invited to volunteer a year of their lives to save the lives of others, and also save their country. Put that way, the Red Cross hoped the invitation would be hard to refuse.

And then the noisy and exciting family Christmas was over. The new marquee in the church yard carried a statement that was almost a threat. "WITHOUT FAITH IT IS IMPOSSIBLE TO PLEASE GOD. Heb 11:6"

Rowenna couldn't pass the church without noting the current sign. She read this one and passed on...she had heard it many times. But wait...is says "impossible to please God." Was there any other place where something was said about another thing that was necessary to please God? Not that she could remember. So what...really...was faith? She'd have to ask Granddad.

The old man nodded. "Now the Bible says the faith 'is the substance of things hoped for and the evidence of things unseen,' but I don't think that's what you want to know. You want a few more words.

"So how about this. Don't worry about what you can't see. God is speaking to his Christians, here, so they know their steps are directed by him if they let him.* Faith is a first cousin to trust. Just let the future alone and God will take care of it, and if we don't trust him to do that, then he is not pleased."

Rowenna nodded knowingly. "Granddad, you explain things so well, you should have been a preacher." That brought a grin to the wrinkled face of the retired minister.

Rowenna thought about the answer as she saddled Mustard. She had made peace with the fact that she would never be a student nurse in a class. There was no reason, really, and it might even be boring. She'd already been there and done that.

But now there was Nathan and his news that should have been a bombshell, but somehow it wasn't. He was going to work on a hospital ship. Maybe. Imagine that!

Mustard was extremely and superbly happy to see her, twisting and head tossing and jingling his bridle loops. He even looked around occasionally as though to make sure she was really there on his back.

Uncomfortable as it was to sit sidesaddle for modesty's sake, she was determined to make the most of this walk. This was one place where the other girl was not looking at her. She was alone with the animal and her thoughts seemed to untangle themselves.

Various of her siblings had been "proud" of her and "puzzled." What a strange behavior for their baby sister. No matter. They loved her and it didn't matter whether they approved. Nothing changed love.

It was New Year's Day, 1917, that Nathan brought the single seated buggy to the hilltop house and picked her up. His pony climbed to the Ridge Road and they rode over the cracked flint of the road bed and under the leafless trees. A cozy afghan kept the draft from knees and sunshine in the buggy was cheery.

There was a strong urge to fill the silences with words, and a firm knowledge that they were not needed. Sometimes more was said without words.

"Nathan...are the other students with you accepting the invitation?"

"Most of them. Some were still thinking. It seemed we were boxed in whichever way we went. A conscription will include us all, and that makes up a mind for sure. There's one thing, of course, and that is I will learn more in that sixteen weeks than I would in a lifetime in Wishbone."

She nodded. "And a lot of it you will never need in Wishbone...but if no one fights for Wishbone, there may be no Wishbone to come back to."

And they rode along. During the last weeks there had been a lot of thought about what to say when Christmas came, but when it was there and they were riding along in the snappy breeze that blew along the ridge, it seemed that all of those things had already been said. The afghan warmed their knees and the wind painted their cheeks, and the clip-clopping of the pony's feet made an afternoon to remember...many times. It painted pictures in the picture book of their memories.

They ended the afternoon with hot chocolate in the diner, and Nathan would leave the next day. He rode the saddled pony to the hilltop house and had a few words with Ma and Pa Moffat and gave them a goodbye. Rowenna followed him to his pony's side, and Nathan circled her shoulders with his arm, drew her close and kissed her...just because he knew if he didn't, he would sincerely regret it.

Who knew what would happen in the next months?

Wally had only a short time to stay. With the singleness of purpose that had always ruled him, he spoke of all he was learning. He didn't speak of the need for volunteer chaplains...as that meant nothing to him. He was just doing what was in front of him, and he would meet the next thing when it arrived.

One very bright spot that illuminated the Moffat family gathering was furnished by Laverne. It took a lot of the pressure off Rowenna for which she was grateful.

In the late summer, the theater had hired a new manager with the impossibly name of Bryce LeBeaux. He had a head full of black curls and an appreciative eye because when he caught a glimpse of Wishbone's gift to the theater…Laverne…he was determined to have her and she was determined to let him. It was actually a good thing that Rowenna had to live at the school, because Laverne's tiny cabin would have been filled to bursting.

Not only that, Laverne had secretly married him in September, not wanting the useless hassle of a big wedding, and now she was roundly and happily pregnant. The whole family was looking forward to June (?) and the grand arrival of another Moffat…even if he must carry the unpronounceable name of his father.

Laverne, of course, had to give up acting when she no longer fit the costumes, but she didn't seem to miss it. The family was, however, concerned that she be without transportation and might be bored, so she was put through a refresher course of harnessing a horse to a buggy. An arrangement was made with a nearby Eureka Springs neighbor to board the horse so there would be a way for Laverne to get somewhere if she wanted to go.

So when Rowenna returned to school, she would take Mustard, Granddad's lonely old yellow horse, and his small, single seated buggy, to be left with Laverne. In this way it would also be there for the times Rowenna could make it home if Granddad did not decide to come over just to visit her.

The last day of her Christmas holiday, this and that happened and she was a bit late leaving Wishbone Hollow. The weak winter sun was setting in the west when she started up the hill, and a bit lower when she reached the Ridge Road. She still had about five miles to go, so it seemed necessary to light the lanterns on the buggy. Then the horse could be more confident as he trotted happily on the flintstone-graveled road.

Mustard turned to watch her as she lit the lanterns, seeming, for all the world, that he could not get enough of the sight of her. She climbed aboard, touched the reins to his rear, and he trotted happily onward.

Dusk had clearly fallen as she was traveling the last mile before turning down into Eureka Springs hollow. She saw the man at the edge of the road with the horse beside him, and trotted on past him. So it was a surprise when she felt his weight on the step to the buggy, and he pushed his way against her, shoving her to the far edge.

Crowded close like they were, she had very little room to move, but he jerked the reins from her hands, and told her, "Lady, I'm takin' this here buggy and you too if you want to go. Or I'll stop this here nag and let you out. You choose."

Rowenna, her hands now empty of the reins, felt free to squirm away far enough for her to maneuver her skirt aside. Practice made perfect, and one lift of the skirt and shove of the hand placed the 22mm Winchester in her right hand.

She lifted the gun and took a shot into the trees beside the road, which only told the robber that in addition to the horse and buggy, he also had a handy little gun to add to his collection. Gathering the reins into his left hand he grabbed for her wrist with his right hand. Mistake!

In the pale light of the buggy lanterns, Rowenna aimed her gun toward his left hand which held the reins, and therefore was more steady. She clenched her teeth for courage and squeezed the trigger.

Direct hit on the edge of his left forearm. The man screamed and released the reins which told Mustard he should do something, but he was not sure what. He knew it wasn't "whoa" so it must mean go "faster," so he did. The old horse remembered how to gallop, and his hooves pounded as the buggy careened from side to side.

In her harshest voice she demanded, "Grab those reins!" She saw the darkness of the red stain spreading on his light colored jacket. "In your right hand…and be quick about it. I still have bullets and I know how to shoot."

He decided that she did, indeed, know how to shoot, so he gathered the reins and tightened them which told Mustard that he no longer needed to gallop so he slowed to a trot.

The robber was not through yet. He tried to cram the lines between his knees to free his right hand. Rowenna saw his intention and wedged her back against the isinglass windshield in the far corner of the tiny buggy space. She advised him, "I don't think you want to do that because I am aiming my next shot just below your belt buckle. If you don't believe me, just try something else."

He seemed to believe her, because the reins were suddenly back in his right hand. His left hand rested against his thigh, still bleeding. She had no idea how much damage she had done but was totally prepared to increase it.

She issued more orders. "Up ahead is the cutoff to Eureka Springs. You are going to turn the horse that direction and make time going down that hill. I think you might need medical help with that arm…like someone to stop the blood."

He prepared to do what she demanded, but she thought he needed encouragement. "I can get you help with that arm, but don't try anything because you have another arm and I can hit it. Right after I deliver the shot below your belt buckle."

Poor Mustard had no idea what was expected of him, but he trusted his girl. He had been with her before when her shots usually brought a squirrel out of a tree, and she had given him no orders…therefore he must keep doing what he was doing. He was quite tired, but when he turned toward town, it was downhill all the way and he must only keep from being over-run by the buggy. Mustard was an old horse, and he remembered a lot of things. Downhill meant "back-off" and tighten his harness against the shafts on either side of him, so he did.

It was a fast trip down the hill and the town was in darkness except for the pale light of the mercury vapor streetlamps. The street was almost empty of traffic, so she had no interference.

Turning her voice toward the buildings she yelled, "Help! Wounded person aboard."

She repeated the phrase and attracted several bystanders. Strong men recognized what was obviously the voice of a young woman in distress, so they ran after her and what seemed to be a "runaway" horse.

At the gate of the hospital, she commanded Mustard to "whoa" which he recognized and appreciated. He lowered his head gasping and panting, his sides heaving from his marathon race. One man grabbed the bridal to calm him, but Mustard gave him no trouble.

The Hospital guard leaped to her side, and readily saw the gun and the direction of the aim. He heard the groan of the man. "It's alright, fellows," he told the gathering crowd. "She's got 'im in her sights, and he's the one that's wounded. Get the police and I can take care of this."

The police, however, had already been notified. Lanterns and searchlights helped the streetlights, and the man, who was in no mood to resist, was handcuffed to a strong officer. Together they walked away. The guard called for the yardman to take the horse to the stable.

Mrs. Cameron and Miss Hollister came pouring out of the building to see that was the hullabaloo.

There was Moffat in her street clothes holding a gun in her hand. Seeing Mrs. Cameron, she quickly lifted the edge of her skirt and slid the weapon out of sight. Mrs. Cameron missed very little. "Moffat, come inside quickly and let the officers handle this."

With clenched teeth and a square chin, Rowenna followed, Miss Hollister bringing up the rear. Suddenly remembering something important, she turned to the men behind her.

"Fellows, there's a good-looking horse tied beside the road about a mile left on Ridge Road. The robber had his horse tied there when he tried to steal my granddad's horse and buggy."

"We'll handle it," came the response.

Rowenna marched bravely on. If she was going to meet her doom, at least the poor horse should not have to pay. She knew the yardman would take care of Mustard until she could get him in the morning. Likely she would be sent home, but what else could she have done…?

She remembered one of Granddad's admonitions. "Whatsoever thine hand find to do, do it with thy might…"** Well, put that way, what her hand found was the little gun in the holster made by her great aunts who decided to help save her life. As she put her foot on the step up to the door, she remembered the rest of the verse that pointed out the obvious "…for there is no work to be done in the grave."

She turned and saw Mustard being led away. He was one wonderful horse and had earned a good rest and a cup of corn! He'd get it, too.

Rowenna was led into the office of Mrs. Cameron. Miss Hollister stayed and no one objected. She needed to know the outcome. The women listened as she related the story, and both knew of the kidnapping she had stopped almost two years before. When she finished the story, she was sent to bed. They'd talk tomorrow, she was promised.

At least she wasn't turned out in the darkness. Amazing, though, that no one asked for her gun. She locked it away before she went to bed. Not much sleep happened, though. She lay awake and wondered. If she had to leave, at least she had her Gold Certificate. Surely that would help. And Pa had bought that little house just behind the aunts. It was still rented, but she could have it…and maybe do…what…? Well, that was tomorrow's problem.

She pounded her pillow into shape and turned over. Then a voice, "Moffat, Nurse Bennett wants you. Now, quickly."

She instantly rolled out of bed as she had been taught was the quickest, safest way. Grabbing up her robe that must be kept close, she slipped it on as she ran down the hall.

An accident. A bloody shirt and a groaning man lay on the gurney. The nurse looked up, "Moffat, get the morphine. We've got a hole to stitch up."

71

Seconds later she was there stretching the skin between thumb and finger for a muscle to inject. A push on the plunger, and he would soon have relief. Then she looked at the whole person.

There, before her, lay the robber. She gasped and drew back. "Moffat, I called you because this is a wound you will often see. I want you to watch the closing and take some of the stitches. Part of something else you'll need to know is that it often happens late at night. So...go prepare the thread while I pick out the cotton shreds of his shirt."

Nodding, she turned to the medicine cabinet and drew out the thread that had been disinfected and oiled. The no-see-ems were killed in the disinfectant, and the oiled thread would pass more smoothly through human skin and be more comfortably removed.

She blocked her fear from her mind and the restraint it had taken to keep from aiming at his head...and later at the spot just inches below his belt buckle. Hatred had no place in a hospital, or in the heart of a nurse. She had done what she had to do, and now she would the next thing she had to do.

She took a look at the damage she had caused. The weapon had taken out a major amount of skin and tore apart a muscle. The shiny white of a bone could be seen among the shreds of flesh. She felt a gagging clutch in the pit of her stomach and she drew a quick breath...that's what the book said to do first. Breath was always needed first. A nurse must not faint.

Then leaning across the man she watched the experienced fingers of Nurse Bennett. Dripping cleansing peroxide into the wound, she quickly sopped it away. Then a spray of iodine from the tiny atomizer. Another blot.

Then the closing began. Somehow the gaping hole was being closed and shreds of skin worked into place. Now the needle....

She had an instant picture of the aunts pushing the needle through the cloth to impress possible customers, looking charming in their lace caps that captured the gray hair above their wrinkles. But now...no lace, no hair and certainly no wrinkles. Pay attention, Moffat, she chided herself.

The needle went in...the oiled thread moved easily. The needle passed through the loop of the knot to secure the end. Then the pulling together. This patch of skin was a part of that one, or, at least, it had been less than two hours ago.

"Moffat, come around here and hold his hand with the thumb turned out so I can better see how this goes." Rowenna moved closer and clasp the hand that had held Mustard's reins and required him to gallop. Swallowing hard, she turned the wrist so the wound was facing the capable fingers passing the thread through the skin and pulling it together the way Ma would pull together a snag of her skirt that she had caught on a brier thorn.

She stared, fascinated. It was truly magic the way the skin reacted. The thread was pulled carefully so as not to pleat or pucker the skin. And then the needle was extended toward her. "Moffat, this is a wonderful time for you to get experience. Take the needle...."

Her hand shook and her whole body trembled. Nurse Bennett looked into her eyes and said, calmly, "Moffat, you must now stop shaking because the needle must be steady. Stop it, right now." Her hand was instantly held firm.

With the tip of a scalpel nearby, the nurse indicated a point where the needle must enter. "Go through the skin and withdraw the needle. Then pull the skin together and stitch under, bringing the thread through carefully. There is no pressure on this wound so you can stitch close. Aim for about an eighth of an inch of skin. Good. Now draw the skin carefully so you don't tear out the flesh."

Word by word the nurse talked her stitches. Rowenna thought, *I'm too slow. When is she going to retrieve the needle and get this done?* But no...eighth of an inch stitches crawled through the torn flesh with the nurse occasionally relieving skin tension by readjusting her grip.

She made her movements pronounced so Rowena could clearly see what was being done. When all skin fragments that remained were stitched together the wound was sprayed again with iodine and patted gently.

"Now we'll bandage," she was told. "Get the cloths and the papers and set them here." And together they wrapped his arm in the soft, sterilized bandages…just as carefully as she and Dollie had wrapped small Lucy's burns.

The man was still, quite under the influence of the sedative. Nurse Bennett positioned his arm beside him on the gurney and covered him with a snowy white sheet.

Rowenna looked at the man…then at the nurse…and sat down on a chair and buried her head in her arms. Sobs arose from the very depth of her being and her shoulders shook so that she could not stop them. Nurse Bennett said nothing but sat beside her until the spasm was over and she had no more tears left to shed.

"Moffat, I let you cry this time, but it will be your last. You will never again allow yourself to come apart this way. It is understandable the first time, but you did your job and that is enough. You do not need tears to drown your fears. Fears never help a nurse and they never go away. Nurses are special people and they do not get to act the way other people act. You will remember this because there will be many times you need to remember it." Rowenna was to remember this admonition many times.

Nurse Bennet put her arms around Rowenna's shoulders and added, "In short, never waste time crying or let tears fall on your patient. You did a good job and I know it was your gun that made this wound. If you had not used your gun, you may have been killed or worse. Now, I want you to go down to the galley where it's warm and wash your face and hands in hot water. Then make tea from whatever kind you like. Sit and drink your tea and remember that you had a lesson in sewing that would have happened sometime, and it was most appropriate that it had happened now. Go…and don't be concerned about what will happen tomorrow."

She did. The warm cloth on her face refreshed her, and the tea was relaxing. She bent over the table for just a second and was awakened by Dollie's hand on her arm. "Rowenna, wake up and talk to me! How was it!"

Rowenna blinked her eyes in a semi daze. "How was what...?"

"On, you ninny! It's all over the school what happened to you?"

And it was on that day that a new rule was made. No gun would be permitted on the premises of the school unless the owner had exhibited extensive knowledge of its use, and when that gun was on the premise, it would be on the person of the owner or safe behind a padlock.

The Wishbone Cryer sounded forth the news.

"The Girl With the Gun has done it again. While taking herself back to school, she thwarted at attack and an attempt to steal her horse and buggy. She left a reminder on his arm that he will never forget. In addition, she was the nurse who stitched him up. How's that for an act of bravery and another one of kindness?"

And the headlines carried the account of the whole incident, blazoned boldly across the top of the paper. Jadeen had been promoted to copy writer/type setter, and she joyfully used up half of the front page of the Cryer in her account.

Not only that, now someone else brought coffee to HER instead of her carrying that stimulant to them.

On the day after the altercation on ridge road, Rowenna wondered if a certain thing should be done. Why not?

She found herself at the door to Mrs. Cameron's office. Should she...? Or should she not...? Oh, well. "Mrs. Cameron...? I want to thank you very much for...."

But the supervisor interrupted. "Moffat, I have no idea what you're talking about. Incidentally, I think you had a birthday... seventeen, is it? I had a newspaper clipping here I thought you might like to see.

Rowenna nodded and took the scrap of newspaper as the supervisor continued briskly down the hall, her starched skirts whispering together.

It was not, of course, a clipping from the Cryer. It was from a St. Louis paper what had picked up a story from an English paper. "The VAT, for female volunteers, is being besieged with girls wanting to help in the war effort. The minimum age for volunteers is eighteen, but it is common information that French girls of thirteen and fourteen are being accepted by the Red Cross if they have the size, and especially if they can drive an auto being used as an ambulance in Belgium. The need for rescue...." And the article went on. Now why did her friend Mrs. Cameron specifically comment on her age and hand her the clipping...?

She was not in France or Belgium. Neither was she eighteen. She folded the clipping to a small square and slipped it down the neck of her white uniform, snuggly tucked into her fitted camisole.

*Proverbs 3: 6
**Ecclesiastics 9:1

ROWENNA AND THE CALENDAR YEAR TURN SEVENTEEN

Sometime during the evening of the incident on the ridge, the yardman had emptied the boot of the buggy of its food offering. Halves of chocolate cakes, thick with icing...a whole pan of gingerbread squares and one of cinnamon/clove spiced apple squares...a pan containing pieces of this and that wedged in together and about a hundred large molasses cookies favored by the children.

These cookies were the remainder of about four hundred that had been baked by Ma over the last weeks before the holiday. Molasses cookies kept forever, it was said, but they wouldn't last long when the student nurses were turned loose on them. In addition, there were three pumpkin pies and three custard pies baked two days ago just for this occasion. Ma was so thoughtful.

The small package of brittle from the aunts was picked up by Rowenna. There wasn't enough for each girl to have a piece and Dollie loved the special attention, anyway.

Buggy boot emptied, it and Mustard were delivered to Laverne by the yardman. A cold, drizzly rain had begun, and he insisted Rowenna mustn't get wet. Everyone was so nice!

During that day, Rowenna was frequently reminded of the clipping in her camisole by one of the corners pressing against her skin. Not painful…just a reminder. Mrs. Cameron was not one to do something like that without a purpose. What did it mean?

As it happened, as Rowenna and Nathan were riding along the ridge in Wishbone, trying to say goodbye to each other without actually saying goodbye, the Chicago Rock Island Pacific railway was chugging through the mountains of Kentucky with a missive that had found its way from England through the government in the east coast. It was headed for Little Rock, Arkansas.

The fledgling US Army Nurse Corp, begun eleven years before, had not yet shaken out their personnel ladder and their intended duties to assist the army. They were, at this time, emphasizing the "assist the military" rather than "being part of the military" but they knew who else they were definitely a "part of" and that was the American Red Cross.

The English commander of the American Red Cross had sent the request to the American counterpart and it was passed through to the infant Army Nurse Corp. Subsequently, OKed and handed back to the Red Cross, it was then dispersed to the various regions of the country.

It was belatedly essential to gather a roster of skilled persons who might be among those who would, for a small pittance, put their country ahead of their own comfort. From the regional director it was broken down and redirected to each registered and approved Nursing School in the country.

They would really like to have…if possible…the names and pertinent information about girls under twenty-five who might be candidates for an overseas assignment. They would like to know the age, general physical size, extent of education and/

or experience and where they had completed certification. Also requested was their ability to converse in the English language. If they happened to have a skill in operating the automobile, it would be good to know, but was not essential. They could quickly be trained.

So far, an adequate number of volunteers had been located for laundry and food service under the older age group. Still needed were those for handling stretchers and the emergency administration of morphine. It was also necessary that they be expert swimmers. The "low countries" of Belgium, Holland and Luxemburg had many canals.

The wheels of government information continued to grind along, and Mrs. Cameron received a letter from her niece who presided over the Memphis Nursing School…and had signed Rowenna's Gold Certificate. She requested her aunt to send along the names and addresses, if possible, of their graduates over the last three years.

The aunt doubted if this would help even if she could find the girls. The mountains of northern Arkansas were so forbidding and the skilled girls had been swallowed up by duties the instant they were graduated, and none were retained by the school. The hospital/nursing school used trainees for everything, thereby furnishing them valuable experience.

She did, however, have contact with one Gold Certificate graduate and that girl now had just received the best warning Mrs. Cameron could give her. The Girl With the Gun was now seventeen, and, while not as tall as they might hope for, was diligent, able to fight her way out of a tight situation and certainly knew how to shoot with the little peashooter gun. Also, she might grow an inch this year.

Speaking of the peashooter, the unsuccessful robber would be in today, and his assailant would have experience in changing the bandage on a gunshot wound and assessing its speed of recovery. After today, he would be sent away and become the property of the law in Fayetteville…a room with bars better able to handle him.

Mrs. Cameron sent her best information back to her niece to include in her own report and included was the name of the Girl With the Gun, along with her own account of the Ridge Road encounter. Also included was a copy of the Cryer with Jadeen's detailed account spread above the fold of that infamous mountain document.

This account was delivered to the Postal Service while Rowenna gently pulled apart the bandage that had been applied so carefully yesterday. While this was being done, his right arm was handcuffed to a chain that was wrapped around the waist of the six-foot three-inch transport agent, Ben War Eagle. Ben's sizeable right hand loosely rested on the grip of the very business-like Colt 45.

While the supervisor looked on, the student examined the wound, still clean, and she looked at the bandage. Only small flecks of blood. She looked at her mentor and heard, "Perfectly normal. Apply a small coating of oil with the brush and re-bandage." With that final bit of instruction, she walked away leaving Rowenna, her attempted abductor and the tall, sober transport agent on their own.

She made herself look up into the face of the robber. The man avoided her gaze and stared toward the window, as soberly as the agent. Applying a clean bandage to his arm, she told herself he was just another patient...of the many she would treat in the future...and then dismissed them to leave through the drizzle of cold rain to the Frisco railway office and the locomotive that would carry him away.

Rowenna had a fleeting thought of his horse that must surely have been rescued and taken...where...? All in all, she had more sympathy for the horse than the man.

The school had a case of the mumps in their isolation ward. No matter. Mumps were not heavily "catching" and most of the girls had gone through them. That included Rowenna, who was taking care of the thirteen-year-old boy. Looking over the food offering in the galley, she decided Ma's lovely custard pie would be a good snack to carry him over till lunch. Currently he was fighting the battle between his appetite and his sore throat. Yes... custard pie it would be good...but first she would have a piece for herself. Ma was good with custard, and the final sprinkle of nutmeg made appetizing designs on the soft cream color of the custard.

A small grin passed her lips as she wondered if this nutmeg was the same she had been sent to the WM for, and had gone also to the diner. Wonderful Ma...so clever and thoughtful. Saw right through her...Ma did...and let her be a puzzled, restless teenage girl... just as she had with Laverne and Jadeen. Ma knew everything would even itself out eventually.

Back at the bedside, she insisted on feeding the boy who was certainly able to feed himself. This way she could offer smaller bites and make it last longer. She thought of a few questions that would keep him talking and not thinking of his misery. The policy was to allow him to stand only to take care of personal concerns. Mumps, on boys, was nothing to be casual about...or so was the general thought. Better be safe than wish they had been.

The cold, drizzly rain also fell on Wishbone. Granddad had donned his nor'easter and leather cap with the ear flaps. Gum boots against the mud and the moisture...he hated wet feet...and with a clean hanky against his sniffles, he headed for the Frisco depot. That was where he could pick up a variety of newspapers not more than two days old.

Knowing the outdoor bench would be empty, he gathered the papers under his nor'easter to keep them dry and headed for the diner. Coffee...! They were making coffee now. Popular demand had made it profitable, and he joyfully produced the nickel for the steaming, fragrant cup and spread the papers before him. It was 1917 and the Britts had dug into their famous white chalk cliffs and implanted fire power to hopefully discourage an attack by sea. Very clever...actually!

Granddad added his mental comments. "Attaboy, limeys. That's usin' the old noggin'!"

The Red Cross had a ship outfitted to head for the English Channel as soon as they got the 'go' word from their counterpart in England. There were a number of American Volunteers aboard…mostly girls. Good Old Red Cross! Trying to get supplies to what was sure to be a battlefield. Ships belonging to the Navy were loaded with necessities gathered by volunteers and low-paid handlers. These supplies were paid for by rich American owners of new companies. The Red Cross still led the way for the much slower American military.

Then the old man's eye re-registered one word on his brain. Girls being shipped away. Girls…? GIRLS! Whose girls, pray tell…? America's girls, of course! Sharp prickles traveled up and down his spine. Girls who belonged to someone…maybe a neighbor. Maybe the one who belonged to him.

Would she…? No, Rowenna would not volunteer as a material handler because she had worked too hard for what she now had. Comforted, to a degree, he still searched the papers.

Doctors! The battle in the channel had conscripted every young man equally, including those with special education and skill. Their well-trained medical personnel had been killed in the trenches and unable to give what their training had equipped them to give. The Red Cross needed doctors, but they were more interested in first aid personnel, those trained to save a life and send them on to field hospitals for further help.

They were looking for young men who had pharmacist training…uh, pharmacist? PHARMACISTS? Wasn't that what young Wilkinson left his papa's market to do? He read farther.

Barbers were also considered as they had a smattering of first aid training, and there were hospital orderlies who, at least, had experience being around and transporting trauma cases. Hmmm, dragging the bottom of the barrel and scraping at the seams, it seemed. The battle was heating up just the way he feared.

Was grandson Wally, John Wallace Hopkins, actually safe in the seminary and how long would he be there? Eighteen and a half, he was now, and strong, educated and intelligent. That would be like waving a red flag in front of the conscriptors. "Drafting," it was called.

He read on. To free up the scarce men for service, girls from France and Belgium were begged for use as ambulance personnel, driving the autos into the battlefields. Girls as young as thirteen if they were tall and strong enough.

Pushing the paper aside, he ordered another cup of the bracing beverage sold for a nickel a cup. There was something he was going to do today, rain or no rain. The trip was going to take at least one more cup of coffee. Wally was miles away but that girl was just down the road a piece.

Still dressed in his weather gear, he hitched Cannonball, the young Appaloosa stallion, to his remaining buggy and headed up to the Ridge Road. Beside him was a sack of peppermint candy known to be a favorite. Maybe he didn't need an offering (reason?) to go see his granddaughter, but it wouldn't hurt.

Rowenna, still being a blue cap had certain liberties if they were not extremely busy. She was puzzled as to why he was here, but he maybe just wanted to see for sure she was safe and whether Mustard had been hurt. She made small light of the altercation on the ridge but Granddad was….

Well, whatever he was, she loved him.

"But, Granddad, I only did what you told me to do. It was him or me that would get hurt, and I decided it would not be me, so I did what my hand found to do. My hand had no trouble at all finding that gun in the little holster the aunts made for me." Her words were issued around the peppermint lozenge in her mouth.

They chatted for twenty minutes and he released her with the bag of mints. He watched her as she hurried as fast as the longer skirt would let her, turned and waved and disappeared within the huge white building. As well as he knew her, he knew for certain that she was the kind who would volunteer if needed. Swallowing the lump in his throat, he turned Cannonball toward the ridge road.

There was nothing he could do with those useless old hands that held the reins and that useless old mind and the faded, nearsighted eyes, to stop her. He might as easily have tried to put a tornado into a bucket and tell it to stay there.

As he climbed to the Ridge Road, the Frisco railway belched forth a breath of steam and smoke and ground its gears for the next hill it was forced to climb. It issued its usual farewell whistle as it cleared the town of Eureka Springs and the sound made a final exclamation point to his fears.

He looked up into the dreary moisture that hid the skies and announced, "God, it's got to be up to you, now. I can't do no more. Would you think on issuin' an extra several angels to watch over that girl?"

If angels care to communicate, they might have said, "Old man, don't you be agitated over that girl. She belongs to us, too, and we're already on the job."

While the Frisco railway carried away the latest information on Nurse Moffat to be given to the Memphis Nursing School, blue cap Moffat was carrying a pail of scalding hot water to the nursery to dip the toys and destroy any no-see-em that might be left by the last child to play with them.

The human/no-see-em battle was never won by either side.

THE CLASS OF YEAR 1917

A select group of twenty-five girls were issued their white caps and scheduled for mornings of classes and afternoons of practical experience. The blue caps were gone, all except for Rowenna.

Rowenna, herself, felt perfectly at home behind the closed doors and found plenty to do unless called to service by someone. A sudden Arkansas freeze-up cold spell flowed down to the valleys and coated every surface with a glistening layer of clear ice. Due to the fact that almost none of Eureka Springs was on level land, there were a lot of slips and falls.

Men with expensive horses were loath to let them out of the paddock for fear of a broken leg. Old folks with brittle bones stayed cloistered behind their doors. Broken arms and a few twisted legs appeared at the hospital just as Rowenna had reached the point of being taught how to set bones…in an emergency. It would be a nurse's duty only if there was no better option, but there would be times in a nurse's duties that she would be the best help available.

Fingers were easy to set, but the thigh bone…? Would she ever get it right because the times a nurse would be required to do it, there would likely be no proper equipment. Then there was the wrapping, splinting and plastering. Those were relatively easy but proper healing did not happen unless the bones with splintered edges were properly put together.

Her arms tingled with tension as she trailed Nurse Bennett's fingers while they sought the extent and location of the break. The older woman whispered, "Finger here…now move down slowly. Feel the bone?"

Fortunately, the patient was feeling no pain, and this hospital was…after all…established for the training of nurses rather than healing the city's ills. Fortunately, both could be handled together, with a bit of patience on both sides. Her hands were guided as the bone was adjusted, straightened and pulled to make the bone ends meet. Feeling for the bone under the flesh was like feeling for one certain feather in a stuffed pillow.

Then came the careful wrapping with the finely cut splints and the whole thing shaped with Plaster of Paris which would harden before the patient was fully awake. The older woman had visions of her young pupil on a hospital ship being "the best that was available." Or worse, on a battlefield headland in a makeshift aid station under the conically shaped tents, fashioned much like the American teepee. One thing was certain, she would do what she could, and this girl would, most undoubtedly, be there eventually and likely before the year was out.

Therefore, they must take full advantage of this famous North Arkansas Freeze-up. There was the old saying that it was an "ill wind that did nobody good." There were three broken arms (easier to set) in the afternoon, a severely sprained ankle and a broken toe. The two broken legs were the next morning and they were from men attending to morning chores with the animals.

On the third day, the ice casings on the twigs were thawing, breaking and falling to the streets, and the underlying warmth was melting the ice on the rocks. Likely no more breaks would occur, but there would be another one or two freeze-ups before spring.

Dollie was among those who received their white caps. She was fortunately academically inclined and she joyfully dived into the classes. Just look, they had pictures in the books that showed how everything looked inside the body…it showed how muscle fibers were bound together in bundles called tendons and could contract to make them work…and it showed the tracks of the veins (nearer the skin and not so important) and the important arteries (usually enclosed in muscles). Very clever the way the body was made!*

The book pictured the important blood carriers that were close to the skin and could be dangerous. Neck. Inside leg. Parts of the chest. And she learned how important the head was. An awful lot of important things were packed into that ball not much bigger than a musk melon from the garden.

It was quickly noticed that Lina, whose mother had been kidnapped and held captive for twenty years, would have a little trouble keeping up. There were so many words she had never heard spoken, as her mother had been only thirteen at the time. But the girl tried hard, sniffing and wiping tears from the effort.

It was about then that Cora noticed the problem. Cora, the big girl who decided if her father was going to make her work, he should pay her. The girl who paid herself from the money in his pockets, giving herself the monetary gifts that paid for her school. One thing her pa had taught her was how to get things done… one way or the other.

Cora took Lina on as a project, and later as a friend, and insisted they study together when they could manage the time. The course schedule called for classes in the morning, so when there was a moment in the afternoon, Cora managed somehow to keep Lina almost up with the class.

In July, the January morning class would be tested and changed to afternoon, to make room for the next morning class. Cora was determined that Lina be part of it, and Lina was eager to accept help from anyone. The girl wanted most of all to make her ma happy, because she had taken such risks for their freedom.

There was something else that was going to bring about a lot of changes in both of the small Arkansas hill towns, Wishbone and Eureka. It was the automobile. The residents had known, of course, that the auto was a common sight on the streets of the big towns, and even Bentonville and Fayetteville had their share and they were increasing. They were smoky, noisy things and didn't look very safe, actually.

Not only that, they were forever stopping for no known reason and requiring the driver to re-adjust something or make arrangements for a horse to pull the contraption to someone who could make the adjustment.

Granddad had looked at the few that made their way into Wishbone, and his mind pulled up the picture of little French and Flemish girls of thirteen actually driving one of the contraptions… that is, if they were tall enough and strong enough.

He pushed away the thought lest he picture Rowenna in one, though his better sense told him she would have no trouble. The girl who pulled a gun on a would-be robber and forced him to drive her to the law by aiming at his belt buckle…that girl would manage. He refused to comprehend that a great lot of her confidence and competence was learned from him.

When she could, Rowenna made the short trip to her sister's cabin and was met practically with tears of joy. Laverne, so accustomed to things going on, was being bored out of her skull. Not only that, her lovely figure was expanding to the bursting point and her happy husband failed to notice how ugly she now was. The whole world could tell, so why couldn't he?

The appearance of a person had never occupied much of Rowenna's attention, but it was an inescapable fact that the pregnancy that should make hair dull had sparked Laverne's with highlights and the wet winter and spring had deepened the waves.

Her complexion took on the porcelain appearance of the expensive dolls that used to be made in Germany before they started making bullets. She had the rosy inner glow that seemed to blossom through her skin. She had nothing, really, to do, so she slept a lot, resting her eyes from her evenings of work. Her eyes were as beautiful and shining as those that artists drew to advertise expensive products.

It must have been her happiness over the baby showing through her skin, and she refused to listen to her sister explain that her beauty was still intact.

One thing though. She was extremely big around the middle...actually huge and getting bigger. Even Rowenna noticed and wondered and kept her puzzles to herself. Checking the wrist as she was trained, her sister's innards seemed to be in excellent shape, so what was the problem? The book said nothing about a pregnant lady actually exploding, and that was a comfort.

She had no pain, but her belly itched. Rowenna located the prescribed cream for this problem, actually the same as was used on the udders of pregnant cows, but she neglected to share that fact with her sister. The ointment helped her belly but not her discouragement over her ballooning size.

And she had a full three months left to go but no one yet had actually exploded. An important fact to remember.

*Psalm 139:14

MARCH OF 1917

While the itch problem with Laverne's belly was being solved, another problem was seeking a solution. The American Director of the Red Cross in England was planning...as the Red Cross did so well...an answer to a problem that might happen. Most likely would happen.

So, with the shortage of first line medical personnel, certain potential working groups were being put together in the almost certain event that they would be needed. It would be an advantage, if they could manage it, to form these groups from the same general locality. America was made up of so many cultures that dialects and word-understanding could present a problem.

A Miss Higbee in England was working on a potential group from the states of Arkansas and Oklahoma…none from Texas in this group, because that state was large enough to form its own. She had received information about a number of girls who fit the objective academically and experience-wise, but this would be narrowed down by those planning marriage. These girls would be so valuable to their family and neighbors, most of them would be settled in and forming their own families before age twenty.

Also, there were those girls who were markedly timid or slow learning and a few that were obviously too small to withstand the rigors of front-line service.

Then there were those who would never entertain a change to their lives after they had acquired the hard-won Certificate of Completion. Bearing this in mind, Miss Higbee was attempting to put together from these unknowns a workable group who would be called up as soon as there was a spot to put them to receive the rudimentary four week training before putting them on the battlefield.

It was her feeling that the designated leader, and every group must have one, should be a Gold Certificate girl if possible, and hopefully have a special skill that would obviously set her apart…and therefore be readily followed. A group of twelve who had strong leadership would present a valuable nugget of service.

With the information she had acquired a month ago, she had built three tentative groups, using only her best judgment of personalities as was furnished by the school where they learned their skill. The more detailed the information furnished by the schools, the more defined her judgment of them could be. Then a remembered sight came before her eyes. Of course!

Popping out from her current list was a seventeen-year-old possessor of a Gold Certificate. Unfortunately she was borderline young but she certainly had a specialized skill. She was apparently a sharpshooter and not afraid to pull the trigger and had actually saved her own life and possibly that of others on separate occasions.

She worked independently and did not require a following. That was not especially good, but if she is a "leader" by nature, she will be followed by others. Miss Higbee knew that, in the best instances, followers chose their leader rather than the other way around.

This girl was not particular about following the prescribed rules and while that could be bad, in this instance, it was actually a plus. What she would be doing was so new to the world that no clear rules existed. Fighting her way out of a hijacking on a country road practically in the dark was a definite plus, and it outweighed the problem of age and also the fact that she was not socially refined. That was the training of many country girls, and would be understood by those put with her.

So...first name on the list, Rowenna Moffat, northern Arkansas.

So next, there was Marilyyn Rudd. She was clearly Welsh from the old-country spelling of her name. It was known all over England that the best male soldiers came from Wales, so why not girls as well? She was five foot five...good height, and she carried a few extra pounds...also good. Finicky eaters had no business being where she would be going. She was also northern Arkansas. She was musical and played the harmonica as well as the fiddle. Definitely a plus. Put her on the list.

Laura Carpenter. Slender built and athletic. Loved cooking and she had a background on native medicines from her family. Would that mean that she had American native strength in her bloodline? Hopefully, yes. Laura worked well with others and was known to assist other students in school. Nothing in her notes to turn her away.

Katie Campbell. Likely Scotch background. Tough and determined, the Campbells fought their wars with the McDonalds and had a record of winning. That couldn't hurt Katie. Katie was five foot four and strongly built. She was reported to be able to play the fife, a favorite musical instrument in Scotland. Katie had a strong, delicate touch when cleaning wounds and she had a cheerful bedside manner. Hopefully her patients would actually have a bed, but there would definitely be cleaning to be done. Certainly every group should benefit from containing a highland lassie.

Helen DuPray. She would be French, very likely. In fact, she spoke the language, though not perfectly. Definitely a plus in Belgium as that small country spoke both French and Dutch. Also a smattering of German. She was also five foot five and somewhat slender, but that should not be a problem. Maybe a plus, actually. There was no way she would not be on the list. She was from central Arkansas closer to Louisiana, but Miss Higbee decided that language skills tipped any other weight on the scales.

Gertrude Ezell. Maybe a bit of German, or more likely Swiss. Rugged people, those Swiss natives. Those who had not migrated mostly had strong feelings for freedom and had filled their mountains with defensive equipment. Maybe some of that fierceness was still within her, and certainly it would be useful. Gertrude scored well but for some reason was not given gold, and in the current circumstances, that was also a plus. One Gold was enough. It was noted that she worked well with others and had several close friends in the classes.

Fannie Gretna. Likely mostly English. She was from the border between the states of Arkansas and Oklahoma. That might make her family recent pioneers. A very good plus…they had withstood a lot of hardships in the settling of Oklahoma. Fannie was five foot six and strong boned, it was noted. That was such a help when such notations were made. Fannie also played the harmonica, likely as a means to entertain herself and family when they were separated from others. She had a family of siblings younger than herself, and her family undoubtedly were counting on acquiring her nursing services. Too bad. Girls like Fannie might help keep the problems on another side of the world, and that would be the best help her family could ever expect.

Carol Gianopolous. Greek. No doubt about that. Her family had legally changed their names to fit in, so she was now actually Carol Gian. She loved to cook and didn't like farm work. Did enough of it, she had announced when she came to school. Obviously she liked nursing because her grades were good. She was jolly and entertaining, and loved being in a group. She might be a leader in certain circumstances if necessary but not to push herself ahead. Carol sounded good as there would be a lot of gathering and preparing of their own food. If the self-contained outpost was set up...as was planned.... Carol would seem to be a plus.

Barbara Reeves. French again, and she spoke French. She was from central Arkansas and it was noted that she was a "peacemaker." Miss Higbee hoped that meant that she settled small disputes that would, for certain, come among the girls. She was five foot three but seemed to have no health problems. Her grades barely cleared the passing point, but she was a good follower and happily attached herself to any group and was not a complainer. Interesting set of information, but Barbara should be a plus.

Rosie Coyote. Oklahoma. She was a runner and was skilled in weaving and painting. She had a knowledge of her family's herbal medicine, but decided she needed more. She has a pronounced dialect but is easily understood. She is a good storyteller and she often entertained the other students. Rosie had been trained to shoot with a bow and arrow, but would rather have a gun, she said.

Twila Screaming Eagle. Oklahoma. Name in process of being changed to "Eagle." She made very good grades, and was loved by the other students. Good natured and willing, her mother's family were Johansson's, likely Swedish background. Her language dialect very understandable. She plays the flute which was not considered something a girl should do, and she follows her own drummer, at times, and has periods of preferring to be alone. It was noted that she had a great sense of fairness.

Ollie Kettle. Originally Yellow Kettle. She knows the Kiowa language and a little French as well as American English. She is five foot seven and willowy built. (Does that mean slim?) Her family members are fishermen and operate their own fishing camp, salting and drying the product, and living in teepee dwellings during the fishing season. She also enjoys swimming and hunting and is proficient with the bow and arrow. She is unusual as a candidate for a Nursing School but she wanted to learn more of what she could add to what her grandmother taught her. She follows instructions with very little help. So Ollie Kettle, formerly Yellow Kettle, was added to the list

Susan Spotted Pony. Oklahoma. Kiowa language. Good education and good grades in both elementary and nursing schools. Very quick to learn and willing to try what she had not done before. (Good trait! If she agrees to go, just about everything she will do will be what she has not done before.) She plays the harmonica and the flute and has won tribal ribbons for her ability to throw a hatchet. (Handy skill assuming she has a hatchet! Could come in handy, though.) She especially wanted the school and loved to study. She was helpful to slower students. She had no perceptible dialect other than southern American. Susan enjoys being completive in games but is well liked. Has earned ribbons in swimming.

Evelyyn Walker. (Eve) Welsh mother. Father from Florida. Original name Fast Walker. She speaks Seminole language as well as some Kiowa. Dialect is understandable, and she understands American English very well. Loves to sing and has a beautiful voice. She is also very attractive and strongly built. (Does that mean muscles or symmetry?) Her father is a skilled carpenter and was the force behind her decision to be a nurse, but she seemed to enjoy learning. Well-liked and sometimes had ideas of her own. (Now what does that mean… doesn't everyone have their own ideas? Maybe they are saying that she could be a leader if necessary but doesn't require a following.) She learned a lot of what she knows from reading the books from the frontier libraries. She acquired a good knowledge of the meanings of words that way. Prefers to be called Eve.

Miss Higbee had spent two whole days going over the information tossed at her, and, sighing with weary satisfaction, she put these twelve names (plus two yet to be assigned) in the packet that would be sent back to the Director of the Red Cross on the east coast. She sincerely hoped her decisions were workable, fitting the personalities, strong points, and skills together along with physical strengths and survivable abilities.

These girls would notified of the Red Cross interest in them in March of 1917, giving them time to get used to the idea and be ready to make a decision by May. She sealed the packet and planted her elbows on the desk, resting her chin on her palms. How unfortunate that she must butt into the lives of these girls who had carefully made plans and, with great effort, had earned their skills.

Oh, well.... War was hell...just like the writer said.

MARCH 1917

All of the student nurses knew of the mail slots issued to each of them, but those who lived close seldom checked for letters. Rowenna was one of those. That is why Mrs. Cameron felt free to mention to Rowenna that she might check her mail slot.

Hmmm, two letters. Wally and Nathan...who would go first? Maybe Wally, her own flesh and blood.

> ...hey, Row, remember when Jonathan's pa bought him that little Roadster auto...and he taught a lot of us fellows to drive it? Of course his main purpose was to ferry Jadeen around, but we learned, nevertheless.
>
> Well, among my college classes was "driving skill" so we all got a chance at the demonstration models. My instructor was so stunned at how fast I learned (I didn't feel like I needed to tell him I sort of already knew) that he told me something interesting.
>
> You know that war that is going on in Europe? They're needing transport pilots to move the aircraft from the factory to the launch sites. They need a lot of them and

my instructor said he'd put me in for one of the slots if I wanted it.

The way I (and the other fellow) see it, we'll be in the war soon anyway. There's no way I can keep out of it. If I go now I can learn to be a pilot. I don't really know what to do, but I accepted anyway. We (the fellows here) are in a position of choosing whether to be shot or drowned or poisoned. Whichever we choose gets us to the same place. I'll know next month, and if I accept I won't get to come home at all, they tell me. You know me, I hate decisions and change but I seem to be rather in the point of the tweezers right now and I feel like I'm the splinter just waiting to be yanked and tossed away. But we (you and I) know what we've been taught and must take it from there.

Another little thing I thought might amuse you. We are supposed to learn a signal alphabet called the Morse Code. It consists of dots and dashes, and it takes forever to say anything. We think it's kind of fun, and we were given little cards to carry while we're learning. I thought you'd like to see them so I'm sending a couple of cards, for you and another of the nurses. I think they are toying with a supplemental code where a certain conformation of dots mean a whole sentence. Maybe like "I've been shot down and I'm injured" or "Send an airplane with explosives to the northwest where there is a cannon nest." I'll try to get more information and tell you.

Row, I really like the idea of you being at that school. I like knowing you will be safe. You share most of my childhood memories and I'd hate them to be lost if something well, we don't know what's going on. Maybe best we don't. Missing you, cuz, I am, John Wallace Hopkins.

Rowenna looked at the two small cardboards in her hand. Looked rather like a game, or a special way of communicating. Sort of fun. *Hey, Dollie would like this…I'll just give her one.*

Then the letter from Nathan. She opened out the folded sheet, and two small cardboards fell to the floor. *Would you look at that! Two more Morse Code cards. How's that for a coincidence?*

And she caught her breath and stood still as a statue. Coincidence. Before her eyes, as clear as if it was a painting, was the church marquee at Wishbone. Two children were performing their regular duty at least once every week. She sorted the letter shapes while Wally placed them on the sign.

…COINCIDENCE: When God decides to remain anonymous….

Finally she could let out the breath. She felt a little bit dizzy…something was trying to send her a message. Somebody, maybe?

Angel…? Are you there? I wish you would speak American. I mostly don't know for sure what you're telling me.

Gently she slipped the letter, still unread, back in the envelope and tucked it up the sleeve of her uniform. The papery surface quickly warmed and the smoothness of the paper against her arm suddenly reminded her of the light pressure of Nathan's hand as he had guided her steps from the diner.

Angel…? Please either go away or tell me what is going on. I don't think I can stand this. And then another picture was before her.* …STAND FAST IN THE FAITH AND BE STRONG….

Those words may not have been from the angel but certainly were "American." She, herself, had sorted the letters out of the box. The words had meant nothing to her then. Now…they seemed to be a stern commandment. Something was going to happen that took effort, like having your feet braced against the push of the wind. Or something worse that was coming at you.

She wore the letter next to her arm for the whole day as she did routine duties. Bringing the towels from the clothesline and folding the piles, distributing them to the various places where they would be needed. She smoothed the clean bandages and passed over each one with the hot pressing iron heated on the kitchen stove. She rather liked that job.

She moved the triangle of iron slowly across the length of the cloth saying to herself, *Die! You filthy no-see-ems! You cannot live here.* Then she grinned at her childish thoughts.

She folded the cloths while still hot and put them in the metal box with a tight lid. Not one no-see-em was going to get inside that box! So there!

Dollie was in class and Rowenna really missed her. She had never had a friend like Dollie who seemed to understand her when she could hardly understand herself. Wally. What was happening with him...and did he write those things to Granddad? If so, poor Granddad.

It was late afternoon before she had the courage to draw Nathan's letter from her sleeve. *Stand fast*, she told herself. *Be strong.*

My dear friend, Rowenna.

I think of you so often, and I love seeing you safe inside that big white box of a building. I want you to be safe forever.

I have learned of a number of changes about to occur. Here in this class of medically minded students there is a lot of talk about the war in Europe and Germany's Emperor Wilhelm. From what we hear, he is determined to carry out the wishes of his generals in their "great rush to the sea." The closest sea would be directly through the lowland countries, specifically Belgium.

I don't want to give you terrible things to think on when you have no way of stopping them, but this is so strong on my mind, I wanted to let you know. For some reason, we are being taught to drive the automobile. It isn't hard, really, and I think of how you would attack this problem. It would certainly be easier for you than most of us, after the way you fended off the robber.

We are being encouraged to volunteer for overseas duty so we will be in place when America enters the war this summer. Every place in Europe needs battlefield medics (that's me they're talking about) but the worse place is where the English Channel narrows at Dover, England and Dunkirk, France, and Ypres, Belgium. If Von Bismarck's army breaks through there and gets to England, the rest of Europe's battles will be of no consequence. We students may be uninformed, but we are not dummies. When the tall grass bends over, we know there is a wind. And the "war grass" is now laying flat on the ground.

A lot of England's energy is going into the new airplanes they're turning out about one every hour, and they think that's the best answer. They may be right, because those observation planes save a lot of lives, but still the battlefields are littered with wounded and dead. The medics cannot get in there until the army makes room. Somehow.

I wanted greatly to have the month at home and to spend time with you as much as your school would allow, but I see that is not going to be possible. This class will be fortunate to even spend our sixteen weeks here. There is talk we will be sent on to England for a "prep" course, whatever that is.

When we were assigned to learn the Morse Code, I thought about you and how clever you were at figuring things out (…me? Clever at puzzles? Who does he think he's writing to…? My whole life is a puzzle I can't figure out!) you might have a moment's interest in the little cards we are now required to carry and memorize. I'm not sure what for, but they tell us they may be necessary for signaling.

My sweet friend, Reena, I apologize for writing all of this to you, but I think, somehow, that you will understand. We are all frightened at what we see, but not one of us has dropped the course. If America makes any mark at all in this war, it will be because of the Red Cross and the brave and wealthy American companies that are funding them.

You are continually in my thoughts. Be strong, my dear.

Nathan.

She read the letter again, every individual word, looking for answers but found none. He sounded scared spitless...just as she was...but he advised her to "be strong." Like "Stand fast in the faith and be strong."

She added the two code cards to Wally's contribution. That meant three she could give away. Dollie, of course. And...well, hey! Cora and Lina! That was exactly who might have a little fun with them.

Dollie was available in the afternoon and was trying to memorize the parts of the body most often damaged...those that the first-aid nurse could easily correct. Rowenna remembered her own time with them, but memory came easy with her. Dollie had giggled with pleasure at the code card. It would be such fun if she ever had a time that she was not wrapped up in her lessons.

It was a night of a full moon, and that surely had nothing to do with Rowenna's restlessness but pounding her pillow had not helped her to sleep. Finally she decided maybe something to eat would help, so she slipped her white robe over her white night gown and went down to the galley.

Quiet and dark, the only sound being the breathing of Ma Gunther, as Lina's ma was called. The woman insisted on sleeping on a folding bed in the kitchen. Keeping the fire going all night was a job no one liked, so Ma Gunther insisted it was hers.

Tiptoeing past her bed, Rowenna checked the warming oven. Various leftovers waited for a hungry student, and a few biscuits were among them. Selecting a biscuit and spooning a spot of fried onions inside, she wandered to the very large, back window where moonlight streamed in. She had a very good view of the back yard including the woodshed, the stable and the kitchen garden. Almost in the center of the garden was the small log cabin for the yardman.

And over in the stable he was, moving about the horses. He was actually in Marshmallow's stall. The huge, beautiful stallion had been a gift to the hospital and he had some sort of fancy name that the girls could not remember and did not like. He looked just like he was made of a huge, white marshmallow, the new treat that the girls dearly loved.

Was there something wrong with Marshmallow? She couldn't imagine what it would be…but the yardman would know. Yardman…? Why was there no light in his cabin if he was tending the horse?

She put her biscuit on the table preparing to step out to ask him, but that was when the stallion tossed his big, beautiful head and his long mane hair flopped, illuminated by the light from the lantern. Something was wrong. Dreadfully wrong. Marshmallow loved the yardman and would even take medicine from him without complaint. That person was NOT the yardman.

Giving Ma Gunther's bed a firm shake, she told her, "Wake up and ring the bell." Rowenna dashed up the stair, took her 22mm from the locker and dashed back down to the kitchen. The cook had woke up, but still thought she was dreaming as she stood beside the Panic Rope.

Every person in Eureka Springs had been schooled about the Panic Rope. It stretched through the four floors of the hospital to the roof cupola and was fastened to a sixteen inch brass bell to be rung for any trouble from a fire to a theft or what-have-you. This wonderful bell boasted two clappers giving it a distinguishable depth of sound.

"Ma, ring the bell! We need help! Someone's trying to steal our horse!"

That got her attention. Pulling with her strong arms, the bell began to clang-clang. Clang-clang. CLANG-CLANG! The whole fourth floor, nearest the bell, was instantly alive and with feet on the floor. *Wonderful, nighttime fire drill*, was their first thought. Shoes on feet and robes in the process of being donned, they thundered down the stairs where every ambulant patient joined them. They scurried out the front door in a river of flowing white.

Rowenna was already at the driveway gate that she knew would have been left open for the escape. She drew the gate closed and locked it and watched the corner of the building. Surely the thief had been tipped off by the clang of the bell and leaped a back fence...or maybe hid in a tree.

But no! Here he came on the back of the white stallion trying to push him into better speed. Now was the time for the report of a gun, just to let him know there was one...and she aimed into the thick willow limbs, hoping they could deflect the bullet. The limbs, however, did nothing to dull or deflect the sound.

Poor Marshmallow! Being forced forward, he cleared the corner of the building and faced the moving river of white, the closed gate and the report of the gun. He did the only thing that nature designed him to do. He bunched the muscles in his strong rear legs and reared, fighting at the air with his front legs.

Instantly, the thief was no longer on his back, so that calmed the stallion a bit...giving him strength enough to whirl around and return to the safety of his stall. That took care of him.

Rowenna saw the thief clearly in the moonlight, his lantern, light now extinguished, was lying bent on the ground beside him. In her sternest voice, she commanded, "DO NOT MOVE. I have a gun and I WILL shoot!"

Actually moving was the last thing on his mind. Circled in flowing robes of white and a jumble of voices he could not understand, he had concerns as to where he really was. He thought it best to remain motionless.

While the circle of white robes closed in for a better look, the yardman, now frighteningly awake and on the job, stared down at the man on the ground. Then, in his duel capacity as reserve security guard, he took over. "Turn over on your stomach while I attach these cuffs."

By this time, neighbors from all directions had answered the school's Panic Bell and were pushing through the white robes to the center of the problem. A pounding of hoofs on the stone street heralded the coming of the sheriff.

Pushing his way through the crowd, he came face to face with the yardman, the now-standing thief and...Rowenna with her "smoking" gun pointed toward the thief. Sheriff Johansson was a tall, rotund man with a full beard and a loud voice. He also had a sharp, quickly-accessing eye.

First was a grin, and then a hearty, guffawing belly laugh. He could hardly restrain his mirth and was joined by the neighbors and finally by the students themselves. About forty-five of them... laughing themselves silly.

Looking from Rowenna and her gun to the yardman and his handcuffed thief, now attached by a belt to his own waist, he was heard to announce, "If I'd'a knowed it was only a thief at the school, I'd'a turned over and went back to sleep. Don't really know why I'm here. The only thing is, I'm bound by law to protect this here horse thief from the Girl With the Gun."

Attaching his own handcuffs to the thief and releasing those belonging to the yardman, he led the thief to his own horse and walked him back to the "pokey." Like Santa Clause clearing the rooftops, Sheriff Johansson shouted as he galloped away, "Go back to sleep, everyone. All is well."

The students, chattering among themselves like a "V" of migrating Canada geese flying overhead, returned to the building and eventually their beds. Dollie had worked her way through the crowd and walked with Rowenna and yardman back to the stable to calm the stallion, still tossing his head and stamping his hooves in agitation.

Dashing to the galley, Dollie sorted through the raw potatoes for one about the size of an egg and dashed back, handing it to Rowenna, who wished she'd have thought of it. On her palm, she offered it to Marshmallow who snorted, tossed his head, and then plucked it neatly from her hand with his black, rubbery mobile lips. An appreciative grumble issued from his throat as he chewed the gift.

"Jolly good!" pronounced the yardman. "Let's go back to sleep."

He did, but the girls did not. Rowenna and Dollie stopped in the galley and lit a lamp. Only two hours until they would have to get up anyway, and they really didn't have much time to talk.

Helping themselves to the biscuits, they toasted them on the flat, iron lids of the stove and spread on butter and honey. The school received a lot of wild honey from the many hives and the multitude of blooming flowers and trees. A valuable sweetening as well as its medicinal use.

Dollie was first. "I get letters from my pa telling me about the war. It scares me and I can't do anything about it. My brother is twenty-three with a wife and baby. Pa's scared he'll be conscripted."

Rowenna chewed, thoughtfully. Should she confide the content of the two letters she had just received? Why not. Who else did she have to confide in? She certainly didn't want to talk with Granddad about this...he could do nothing but worry.

Two hours later Rowenna and Dollie began to realize they were more alike than they could ever have imagined. They were practically finishing each other's sentences.

"Dollie, what's going to happen to us? I keep feeling that all my plans to go back to Wishbone are not going to happen. I seem to be walking down a path that suddenly drops into nothing."

Dollie nodded. "And maybe like we end up somewhere and doing something that is nothing like what we ever did...or saw. It's scary."

Rowenna buttered another biscuit. Her third. She sighed and watched Dollie's serious face…the serious face that looked so out of place on this good natured, jolly friend. Dollie continued.

"How soon does your boyfriend say he'll be sent over…?"

Boyfriend…? Nathan…? Well, his letter had sounded as though he thought he was. At seventeen, Rowenna had never really considered it. Too busy.

"Well, he says he won't get a leave, and that it could be at any time."

It was that morning that a decision was made by the Red Cross Medical Detachment in Fayetteville. Their volunteers would be sent to England for last minute instructions and be prepared to come ashore at the Somme River mouth to set up an aid station. It would maintain an ambulance corps and would attempt to serve Belgium's wounded.

If the army could clear and hold that position, it would give the medics a base to work from, rather than out of the inconvenient hospital ship. There was no spot available, as yet, but the English had firm plans, and an iron-clad determination. They had no other way to go.

Accumulating Nathan's education, experience in store management and progress in the sixteen week preparedness course, he would clearly qualify for officer statue just as soon as America entered the war. He, at age almost twenty-two, would therefore be temporarily in charge of the Somme River Camp.

He had been sent to driving school and had learned quickly, and that was necessary. The Somme River Camp would be the discharge point for barge traffic upriver when the shelling permitted. The seriously wounded would be sent to the hospital upriver, if it kept from being over-run by the enemy. Mules or motor launch would pull the barges upstream and getting them back would a matter of setting them afloat.

The fighting in the channel was adding emphasis to the Somme River Camp, which would eventually be a Medical Detatchment (MedDet). The channel could become a battle in hours with the activity of the German Albatross and its improved abilities. The German U-boats attacked the shipping from underwater and that resulted in great losses. The whole detachment would have to be ready to evacuate within minutes.

There would need to be a facility for the horses to have them ready for use, and it would need be on the Belgium side of the river. Somewhere among the volunteers would be a horseman and he would likely be from the Midwest. He could work in conjunction with Captain Wilkinson in bringing the wounded to the medics.

Then a third person would need to be capable in repair of the various vehicles that were donated for use as ambulances. Those skills would be an important determining factor as to where mechanics were stationed and Somme River MedDet would be on the top of the list.

It was the day of the aborted theft of the white stallion that uniforms were issued carrying the Red Cross insignia. Nathan looked in surprise at the silver first lieutenant bars on his shoulder. The "powers that be" had seemed to think it best to go this way, and the bar would later be exchanged for a captains. This would give him a graduation which would be better understood by those under him.

The Mechanic and the Animal Officer would be Lieutenants and under the structure (actually, on loan) until the US Army was official and in place. A lot of valuable time would be saved in this way.

It was a relief that there were enough highly qualified volunteers to make these selections possible…and by late April they should be on the ship.

*I Corinthians 16: 13

WISHBONE CRYER, WISHBONE

Jadeen was soaring in her best element. The Girl With the Gun had furnished more copy.

The printing run of the Wishbone Cryer was quadrupled in its first edition and the fame of this paper was likely to reach Fayetteville and possibly even the capitol city, Little Rock.

Jadeen, nineteen-year-old sister of the Girl With the Gun, could attribute much of her meteoric rise within the publishing of the paper to said sister, who regularly furnished interesting material.

How information can travel so fast would puzzle an outsider but was commonplace to the natives of Northern Arkansas. It passed from mouth to mouth with instant rapidity and stories could climb over ridges and crawl through hollows in a matter of hours.

One might think this would make the printed papers redundant, but that does not happen. There is always the desire for the printed word to compare with what they heard and what they thought they heard. And at times, added to before they passed on.

It became known that the copywriter of the Cryer was a real pack-rat for sniffing out activities of interest, and she had a wonderful record for printing the actual truth. The growth of the paper had doubled with her job promotion.

The headlines above the fold stated that the Girl With the Gun was at it again, and her guardianship now extended to horses.

"GIRL WITH THE GUN SAVES MARSHMALLOW FROM THEFT"

A convenient item of interest was the ability to explain that Marshmallow was actual a horse, and not a condiment to be roasted over a flame. The account explained that the shooter had only desired a midnight snack and had accidentally witnessed the attack in progress.

It went on to tell of the nurses in white nighties and robes flowing onto the lawn to obey what might be a fire drill...or something worse. But it was only a problem already taken care of when the sound of the gun frightened the horse to buck off the rider onto his rear end where he was cuffed by the yardman.

And more details followed.

All of the papers were sold, and most of them went through more than one person's hands. This was about the most fun from a story ever produced, and it was cleverly worded by their own Jadeen Moffat about her sister, the acclaimed Girl With the Gun. If Jadeen had not already been promoted, it would have happened at this time.

While in Eureka Springs, the Girl With the Gun spent some time hidden in the corner of the galley, cleaning her gun after use as Granddad had insisted. This was while Granddad basked in the reflected glow of being the grandfather of the girl who saved the valuable stallion that was given to the school to pull their solid white wagon for a funeral when requested. The fact that the animal "ate like a horse" was not a problem, as the school often received gifts of hay or chopped corn designated for that animal.

Granddad's pleasure was short lived, however, as he continued to read the papers. He promised himself regularly that he would quit buying something that gave him so much sadness. No matter. He was addicted. He would buy papers. He could see clearly that the outside world already had Wally, and could Rowenna be far behind?

And Rowenna, herself, had concern for her sister. A near as could be counted, she had safely cleared the seventh month… with her as beautiful as ever, except for the ballooning of her waistline. Simply rising from a chair was an effort, and preparing food was an impossibility. She could hardly see her shoes when she stood or reach her feet to put them on when she sat.

Rowenna had very little time to help, and her husband picked up whatever duty was left, but she became so discouraged she spent days alone, crying. She had instructions to yell at a neighbor if she began to feel pain, but it was only boredom and discouragement that distressed her. So far.

Rowenna was certain that she was carrying twins, but her sister didn't want anyone seeing her, not even a doctor. "You are going to deliver my baby," she announced to Rowenna. "You have a lot of experience. You can do what had to be done. I don't want anyone else touching me and the baby."

Rowenna hadn't the heart to tell her that was not wise. She felt that she might need all the help she could get, and she confided her fears to Mrs. Cameron who listened with concerned interest. She understood completely and was sure Rowenna was not overplaying the danger.

"When she comes in, we will alert the second semester class. It will be an occasion for learning for them, if nothing else, and help if we need it. When labor actually starts, she won't care if it is the gardener himself who touches the baby. Trust me on that, Rowenna, dear."

Rowenna was comforted. The older woman's use of "Rowenna, dear" instead of "Moffat" was a sure sign of that. At this point, each day that went by was a plus, and Rowenna was "spared" often to perform a little sisterly duty such as a bath.

LAVERNE'S TIME

It was a private little joke between the sisters. "Am I to be forever giving you a bath?"

Laverne would chuckle and nod. "Or you could just leave me to smell bad and embarrass your friends when I go in." Laverne's appetite was practically non-existent. It was almost as though there was no room in her abdomen for food. Rowenna went back to the applesauce with cinnamon as often as she could. Toast and cheese, sometimes.

She reached the first week of the eighth month, and her discomfort became pain. Her distraught husband eyed the height of the buggy step and knew she could never make it. He was quite experienced in handling wood, as theater scenery was forever being needed, so he appropriated thick boards ten feet long and fastened them into a platform slanting from the ground to the buggy seat.

Next he positioned Granddad's small buggy beside the sloping board and chocked the wheels to make them solid. There. It was ready. With care she could walk up. Maybe. Surely he could lift her down when he got her there.

It was only days later than she woke him in the night and told him she was being attacked by a knife and she was afraid it would hurt the baby.

Attacked with a knife…? What the… Oh, Dear Gracious Lord, she was talking out of her mind. *What shall I do?* Then… idea…!

"Laverne, sweetie. I know what to do. We'll get away from that old knife. I have a way all fixed and just let me hitch old Mustard and we'll leave."

Hitching done, he came for her and she was on the floor. Drenched and soggy. Taking her robe from the closet he inserted her arms while she looked at him with a puzzled expression. Then she asked, innocently, "Who are you?"

The quick-thinking Frenchman told her, "I'm an angel and I've come for you." He watched her face. Small smile.

Then, "Whoever you are, don't forget to bring the baby."

"I have the baby taken care of. Now we have to get you on your feet so you can get in my chariot." That was more easily said than done, as it took his whole strength to get her up to the bed, and then to her feet.

Small steps…hold to the walls…encourage her to take another step. Then through the door. In the light from the kitchen window, she saw the "chariot."

"I can walk up there." He sincerely hoped that was true, and it was slow, but eventually she was seated.

Mustard reacted in his usual efficiency, and they rolled down the street toward the hospital. Laverne had a lot to say and none of it made any sense. Bryce was beginning to be very concerned. When he saw the mercury vapor lamps in front of the building, he sighed with relief.

Halting Mustard he told Laverne to sit still and he would be back. She asked where he was going, and he told her he to open heaven's doors for her, all the while hoping fervently that it was not so.

The night watch nurse met him, saw the problem and took the stairs three at a time lifting her skirt to make that possible. "MOFFAT! Your sister's here! Wake up."

Rowenna rolled over and into her shoes. Grabbing a robe she told the nurse, "Wake Miss Gardner. Wake Nurse Bennett. Is the wheelchair ready?"

"Yes!" she yelled as she disappeared.

Rowenna bounded down the stairs, night gown and robe tail gathered to her waist for speed. Pushing the high-wheeled chair toward her brother-in-law, she ran to the buggy. She was met with the pleasant words, "Are you an angel, too?"

Rowenna felt her heart drop into her feet. Out of her head. Unconscious...actually. She forced her voice to be pleasant. "Yes, I'm an angel and we're going to take good care of you. We're going to help you into this big chair and give you a ride." Was she understanding anything?

"Thank you, angel. Remember to get my baby so it can go to heaven with me." Like her brother-in-law, she prayed, *Oh, dear gracious Lord, do help us! Is she going to die? What is she seeing? I can't...oh, I can't....* all the while knowing she must.

Bryce climbed into the buggy behind Laverne and caught her under the arms, gently turning her. Rowenna guided her legs toward this wonderful chair made for just this action. The back could be made to slope at various heights. The patient seemed to be in absolutely no pain, though the reason for that was too horrible to consider.

Firmly on the board seat, Rowenna raised the chair back and began to push. Projecting ahead, she was sincerely glad for the pulley operated elevator. Guiding the chair into the small box, she entered and Bryce crowded in beside her. Together they pulled the rope that easily lifted them to the second floor.

The door was open and all three of the requested ladies were there. Laverne was wheeled into the birthing room and removed to the bed. There was no way she could use the birthing chair in her mental condition, so they were going to have to have strong arm help.

Rowenna shouted to the watch nurse. "Go wake Cora. I need her."

Midwife Gardner approached to examine her and Laverne went of fit of hysteria. "Go away! You're hurting me with your knives and you're trying to hurt my baby!" She flailed with her arms and kicked as well as she could under the sheet.

Cora stepped in the room followed by the entire second semester class. She cast her look around to see why she was called.

Rowenna was on her knees by her sister's pillow trying to calm her. "Sis, there's another angel here to help you. She's going to help you sit up."

Now Cora knew what to do. She was to be on her knees behind the patient, allowing her to lean back but be held firmly under the arms. This position was thought to activate the birth muscles and remove strain from the other parts of the body. It seemed to work. Sometimes. Laverne allowed the other "angel" to do what she needed to do, but screamed when any of the ladies approached.

The student nurses crowded closely as possible without agitating the patient. This was something they certainly wanted to see…they might have a need of the information. They were right.

Rowenna had relinquished her space to Cora, who was not a small person. She easily held Laverne in the proscribed position, and Rowenna dipped a cloth in the warm water that conveniently appeared close by. She gently wiped Laverne's face, smiling and talking to her…being scared out of her wits but refusing to allow herself to tremble.

"Here I am bathing you again. How does that keep happening?"

Her sister giggled quietly, ladylike and then cast her eyes around the crowd of people in the room. Her eyes widened and she screamed as loud as a human voice can scream and yelled. "Go away! Go away! You're hurting me!"

Nurse Bennett slipped around and approached beside Cora. "Rowenna, I think she's coming to. She's feeling pain so I think you should see how far along she is."

Of course! How could she have forgotten that? So concerned for her sister, she forgot the baby. Babies!

Drawing back the sheet, she saw the pair of tiny feet. Adjusting her sister's leg, she pulled up her memory of the pictures in the book. Place hand on baby's back and guide. Feet first not good. Turn slowly to have baby's chin to the side.

On her knees on the bed, she bent toward the small struggling body. She had a fleeting appreciation of her first observation when the patient, Emily Parnell, was flat on the floor. Seemed easier. Baby was warm and slick. How tight was it safe to grip him? A shoulder appeared...then an arm.

NOW! The care of the chin. Baby was turned sideways and he began to yell. Where was the other arm? Ah! There it was!

In her relief she told him, "I'd yell, too, little fellow."

And there he was in her hands and a folded towel appeared beside her. Baby on towel. Done! Wonderful, but Laverne was still screaming. Rowenna had been so intent on the baby, she had not noticed. She prepared to back away and step down from the bed, and she saw the top of a tiny head.

WHAT was going on! She had thought all along there might be two, and now she had forgotten. What a dunce she was! Pulling up her memory she scanned the words. Headfirst good. Nose and chin tipped the right way. In side vision she could see hands working with the first baby as she turned the small face this way and that allowing the tiny shoulders to emerge. Home free!

She slid the tiny form onto her palms. Screams of indignation blended with those of her mother. Another folded towel appeared and she placed the little girl on it. Hands and clippers were working around her with the screams of the mother drowning out conversation.

She moved her position to reach her sister's abdomen, and something emerged. It looked like...oh, no, it couldn't be! Another baby and it was dead! Back in midwife position, she received the warm, silent body. No! Not now! Not after what Laverne has gone through!

She looked up, tears streaming. "Angel, please don't let this happen."

Her mind saw the printed words. Baby silent? First scratch lightly on foot soles. She did. Nothing. She looked again at the mental picture. One hand under baby's shoulders. Fingers press chest…let up…press again. Turn baby head and check mouth.

Nurse Bennett was hovering beside her, ready to help. Baby's mouth emptied. Tiny hand jerked…didn't it? Back with four fingers against the tiny chest. Push…let up…push…. She dashed her sleeve against her own streaming tears. She pled, "Whichever angel guards this little girl, we need you."

"Rowenna, baby is breathing. You can stop now."

Rowenna did not see the student nurses looking at each other. What is she doing?

Midwife Gardner stood by Cora, still in her position. "Lay her down now and she can have the morphine." Cora worked her cramped knees to the floor and stepped away. Within a minute Laverne's voice was quieting and was finally silent.

Rowenna looked around the room at the observation gallery. She had seemed unaware that they were there. It was over. She felt like drooping down on the bed beside her sister, but instead she continued the duties of a midwife. She had observed many births and knew the routine. With a fresh cloth and water, she cleaned her sister yet one more time, and drew up the sheet.

She looked around. Three babies. Boy and two girls. All done. Laverne actually HAD been about to burst. Terribly small, these babies. They would for sure have to stay at the hospital for at least two weeks. That would let Laverne have some rest. It was a good thing her husband had been at home.

Husband? HUSBAND! Oh, the poor man! All that screaming and then the silence? What must he be thinking! Washing her hands and drying them on one of the snowy white folded towels that she may have folded, she walked down the hall to the tiny waiting room. She saw her brother-in-law with both hands clasped above his head and leaning on the wall.

"Bryce...? It's finally over."

"WHAT'S OVER?"

Oh, dear, he had been worried about Laverne's life! "Bryce, she's fine. She had a very hard time and she will have to sleep for a long time. But no matter what you heard or thought, she did fine. You have babies."

"Babies...?

"A fine boy and two beautiful girls. Are you ready for that?" She smiled happily, ready to enjoy his pleasure.

The normal tan of his skin faded as his knees gave way. He crumbled gracefully to the braided rug before the waiting room settee. She stared aghast and unbelieving! He had fainted!

She heard Dollie's voice behind her. "I'll get the salts." And in a minute she was back, handing the bottle with the strong smelling substance toward her. Rowenna knelt beside the stricken man and waved the ammonia before his face.

He startled, shook his head, looked up at her and struggled to sit up. Dollie offered a hand. He looked at Rowenna and shook his head, "I really don't think I can...."

"Don't think about it, Bryce. You already have." Dollie burst into her signature giggles.

Rowenna continued, "But you don't get them yet. They're very small and Laverne can't leave either. I'm certain she can't go home for a week, at least. She's had a very hard time and needs rest. In an hour or so, you can see the babies. One of the nurses will sit the night with them, but they're all breathing. Just remember that."

He picked himself up from the floor and moved to the settee. "Well, I."

"Bryce, I'm certain the yardman has taken care of Mustard. Why don't you just stretch out on the settee until morning? Your clothes can't get messed up any worse than they are now."

Eureka Springs had sort of a messenger service that would deliver important messages to the next hollow or two, for a fee. Rowenna took a sheet of hospital stationery and wrote:

Laverne delivered and is now resting. Three babies are in the nursery. You can see your grandbabies any time and be sure to tell Jadeen. The whole world will want to know. Came at least six weeks early.

Bryce fainted when he heard there were three. I wanted to tell him we could maybe put a couple of them in a sack and drown them in Little Mulberry, like some people used to do cats, but I didn't think he could take it. No names yet. My love, Thirteenth Kid."

She'd take it to the messenger in the morning, but now she was hungry. What was in the kitchen? Smelled like hot chocolate. Strange.

She stepped into the galley and saw Dollie at a table with two thick mugs. "What took you so long? Sit down and I'll pour."

Rowenna slouched into a chair. Exhausted. Drained. And here was Dollie. How had she lived her life so long without a friend like Dollie?

The chocolate was rich with cream and sweet with honey. It filled her throat in the most wonderful way. "How did you know I was coming down here?"

Dollie just looked at her as though she didn't understand the question. "How could I not know?"

Then she continued, "Oh, Rowenna, you did such a wonderful job. Cora woke me because she knew I'd want to be there. They let me get the hot water for the babies. You were so brave when your sister wouldn't let anyone else come near. Just imagine! Triplets!

"I know you said she thought she was going to burst, but almost every pregnant woman thinks that. Your sister really was! What if she had to wait another month? When she was talking out of her head, we were all scared, but it was like the birth pain actually brought her mind back. This is something I will never forget." She paused and studied her friend.

"And the angel, Rowenna. What was that all about?"

Rowenna drained her drink. "I'll tell you tomorrow. If we can find a Bible, I can show you.* Angels are assigned by God to take charge of people. I thank you for the chocolate and for the help upstairs. I think my angel is trying to put me to sleep."

They walked up the stairs as the hands on the clock proclaimed it to be 3:00 o'clock. AM.

The Wishbone Cryer did its part. Jadeen chose the right-hand column rather than the above-the-fold headlines.

The Girl With the Gun

Our hometown girl makes headlines again. Yesterday she delivered triplet babies at the laying-in hospital in Eureka Springs.

A little boy and two little girls made their appearance into their auntie's arms as she delivered these babies for her sister, Laverne, well known to movie goers all over northern Arkansas. The babies came a bit early but their delivery nurse had help standing by, and they all survived and are breathing well, though they remain a trifle small. No matter.

There was a slight mishap when the babies' papa was advised that there were three of them. He took a dive to the rug but the ammonia bottle brought him around. He, also, survived and is breathing normally.

The babies' small size will be no problem. When Grandma Loretta Moffat slides the babies up to her table, they'll pick up weight very fast. Nothing can get her down after her thirteenth kid delivered her eleventh kid of three babies at one time and here's the twelfth kid to tell the world.

The whole family is bearing up well, and we appreciate all your good wishes.

*Psalm, 91:11

AMERICAN DECLARATION, APRIL 6, 1917

The special nurse for the triplets and their mother was, of course, Nurse Moffat. She was assisted by Student Nurse Duffy and Nurse Cora Miller who assisted at the delivery.

Head Nurse Bennett issued a few orders on her own. The mother was not to be allowed to be up from bed, except for small necessary exceptions. She would not be permitted to walk to the chamber room so the necessary article was delivered to her bedside, and the curtain drawn when it was in use.

Laverne must not be permitted to strain in any way for at least two days, and that meant she must be attended by a nurse during these private moments. Rowenna's strong arms supported her sister as she eased from her bed, balanced her against a wave of dizziness, then lowered her to the container, and the sisters looked each other in the face and burst into a fit of uncontrollable giggles.

"Sis...haven't we done this before...?"

And Rowenna, holding her sister's shoulders securely upright, replied between giggles, "Yes, I believe we did this just last year. I must say you look better now than you did then."

Her sister replied, "And you also look better. I couldn't see you then because you had the shades drawn and I spent a month in the dark."

Bottles must be prepared for the three newcomers and Dollie and Cora were happily drafted for the job. They carefully measured the formulae and noted the amount each baby took, only there was no way to be truly accurate. The babies' mother nursed them, one baby this feeding and another one the next time. This situation of mother's milk production might get better and it might not. No matter. Those babies were half Moffat and the Moffats could do anything.

They were held in the hospital for a full three weeks, mostly to be used as lesson material for the class that would be graduating in December. They were the ones in the observation gallery during the actual delivery.

On the 6th of April, 1917, Mustard brought the buggy to the hospital and carried them and their proud mother home to the little cabin. Papa Bryce insisted he could take it from there, so Rowenna stood at the window and watched them go. It was then that her weariness began to settle in, and she felt wilted as a daisy out of water on a summer day.

The personal mail slots were beside the door so she glanced that way and saw something in her slot. Hmmm, two letters... no three. How about that? There was Wally and Nathan, and that other one from...what is this all about? The American Red Cross. Obviously there was a mistake...so she set it aside.

Wally's note was short. An unexpected opening occurred with the Royal Flying Corps and he was accepted as a trainee. He had to leave immediately and was going to board a ship momentarily.

He regretted the shortness of the information, but he would fill her in later. He just wanted her to know where he would be in case she tried to contact him.

As the strangeness in her life continued, she learned that Nathan would be on a ship by the time she received the letter. He was being positioned by the Red Cross and set up where he would work but would be transferred to the Army as soon as America entered the war.

He wished he could tell her more, but that's all he knew now, except that he would be in England for about a month for last minute training. He would tell her more when he knew it. He was glad she was safe in their wonderful state of Arkansas, and he would be there as soon as he could. Meanwhile, he would remember the last days they had together.

Then there was that other letter, and it was clearly addressed to her at the school instead of at home. Hmmm, well, she'd just look at it.

Dear Miss Moffat,

Our congratulations to you on your completion of the basics of nursing, and that you did so with honors. That is why we are contacting you.

Your country is badly in need of the skill that you and your associates have earned though so much study and labor, and we have hoped you would be able to give a few patriotic months in this capacity.

We have chosen twelve other young ladies who have recently completed certification, and are seemingly not encumbered with family duties or responsibilities. We would like to place them with you as a working team to assist any wounded civilians in the war zone, and also the soldiers from either side of the battle.

This assignment would be overseas near the English Channel. Every possible precaution will be made to create a successful working environment for this group, but the assignment will, of necessity, be near the battle front.

Please give this your most devoted consideration, and if it will be possible to give your government this gift of your time and skill, please make a note of such on the reverse of this letter and slip it into the enclosed, postage paid envelope.

God be with you,

The American Red Cross

Rowenna had read each word carefully...breathlessly... her heart seeming to pound harder with each minute and each additional word. She felt the perspiration break out on her head, and her knees turn to jelly. She slid down to the floor, her back against the wall with the letter in her lap. The furniture in the room seemed to be trying to circle around the walls, and the floor wavered and undulated like the surface of Little Mulberry River in a spring flood.

She spread her hands to the floor on both sides to steady her body and she was in that position when Mrs. Cameron came by. Rowenna weakly picked up the Red Cross letter and extended it toward the older woman.

The older woman took the letter and read it, and did not seem surprised. "Rowenna, honey, let me help you up and we'll go to my office." And she extended a hand, gratefully accepted.

Seated, she faced her mentor, hoping for an explanation... or perhaps a reprieve. What seemed to have happened could not, of course, really be happening.

"My dear, I knew this was coming but I did not expect it so soon. I wanted you to enjoy your time before you had to make a life-shaping decision. I wanted your sister to be delivered, and that has happened, and there is never a good time for news like this. Every young man will receive a letter, and it will be a command. Yours is an invitation.

"I might mention that the Red Cross has had their eye on you and a number of others since the first of the year, and with your record, you were sure to receive the letter."

"My record...?"

The nurse nodded. "A Gold Certificate is hard to hide in the nursing community. It indicates that you exhibited various traits or abilities above the basics of healing. For one thing, you have saved your own life at least twice, and that is likely known by them. This is a very important job, and not every girl will be invited. Your letter came alone to the school because you are the only one we have just now who has completed the course.

"I wish I could help you with this decision but I mustn't, and I would not if I could. You are well able to do this alone. You might talk with your grandfather and use his wisdom along with your own, but the decision must be yours."

She paused. Rowenna sincerely wished to produce words that somehow made sense but the sounds were stuck behind the lump in her throat. She couldn't possibly do this. Surely it was obvious to everyone. Here she was the thirteenth kid of a mountain family in the rock-studded state of Arkansas. How could the "powers that be" have managed to learn about her?

Somehow, two mugs of tea appeared in Mrs. Cameron's office. Beautiful Dollie, with a sad smile, turned and left in a whisper of starched uniform. How did she know…? What talent was it that Dollie possessed, that so often seemed to put her where she was needed…? And fit so well…?

Mrs. Cameron had smiled thanks at Dollie, and turned to her steaming mug, its fragrance filling the room. "Rowenna, my dear, it's just that you are the first. There will be others. Our nurses have such valuable skills that they will be discovered quickly. They will be forced to make this same decision. You must remember that you have a special talent that puts you where you are needed, and that has happened several times."

Rowenna gratefully wrapped her cold hands around the warm mug, even though it was a radiant and sunny April day. Arkansas could be so beautiful in April. She sipped the bracing taste of peppermint with a touch of peppery spice from the hibiscus blossoms that ringed the garden fence. Blossoms that were carefully gathered by Ma Gunther and dried for her "girls."

Red Zinger tea, she told the girls.

"Rowenna, dear, you must take a trip back to Wishbone tomorrow and spend time with your family. This affects them, too. Isn't your favorite horse at your sister's house? She won't be able to use if for a while. Go, and talk with your grandfather. Did you get other letters…?"

The older lady wished to soften the blow, but that was not to be.

Rowenna held up the two letters and nodded. "One from my cousin, and he's on a ship headed for England. The other from my…from my boyfriend, and by now he's on his way, too. My cousin is going to fly one of those dinky little airplanes and my…boyfriend…he's going to be a battlefield medic…whatever that is."

Mrs. Cameron wilted into her chair. Such terrible timing, but perhaps this is better. This girl can deal with the whole load if she just has time. She must! She watched as the girl drained her tea, squared her shoulders and reached for the other mug. "I'll take them to the kitchen. Thank you for listening."

And she walked away. Mrs. Cameron lowered her head for a moment onto her arms and moaned. *What are we doing to our children?* Then she sniffed, squared her shoulders and left her small office.

Rowenna had been sent to her family so she walked to Laverne's. The sisters cried together, and the held the babies, marveling at their sweetness. Still too tiny, but Laverne seemed to have things under control, attending to nothing but the babies who were a full-time job.

Still in her white uniform, Rowenna harnessed Mustard to the buggy and he happily tripped along the street to the ridge road, then trotted onward, tossing his head with happiness to be of service to his favorite girl.

Granddad first, before she climbed the hill to her parents. He read the letter and looked at her. Then he read it again. "Rowenna, I suppose you have noticed that you will be the leader of this group."

"No, Granddad. I am number thirteen...again...that's what it says."

The snow-white hair and the wrinkled face shook slowly back and forth, the faded eyes boring into hers. "It says that you were chosen for your Gold Certificate status, and the other twelve girls have completion certification. They were explicit on that. They have selected twelve others they will 'put with you.' You are not reading every word, Rowenna. I've told you about reading every word when you read the Bible. The Red Cross is clearly telling you they have carefully considered, and are of the opinion that you can act as group leader on an important mission. No matter what you think they said, you will see I'm right on what I'm telling you.

"You need to remember that while you decide. They feel that you are just 'a cut above' and therefore you can deliver service that is 'just a little more.' I agree with them, but it is your decision that counts. You are your own worse critic, and that is good, but you must remember each word…that is what you must do."

If Rowenna had expected sympathy, she didn't get it. She left Granddad with a clearer picture of what was ahead, and Granddad watched her through his window until he could no longer see Mustard's yellow pelt. Then he knelt at his easy chair and, tears streaming from his faded eyes, begged heaven to send extra angels to uphold the girl who was climbing the hill to break her parent's hearts.

Ma and Pa were stunned. Just when it seemed things were leveling out, something else happened in the life of their thirteenth kid. Like Granddad, they insisted the decision was hers, and she must think of the possible consequences if she accepted…or if she rejected…this "invitation."

She entered her old room, the room that belonged to that other girl and certainly not to her. She looked at the books on the wall bookshelf. All ten of them, and the medical dictionary along with the gift book of common diseases. They were where her strange path started. No, that was not true. They were just a step upward. It was not even Florence Nightingale who was the first step. Maybe it was Granddad, but it didn't matter now. She was already several steps up the ladder and must climb or descend. Her decision….

She was now seventeen and a half years old. Girls grew up fast in the mountains, and the war was making them grow faster. She knew, deep within herself, what her decision would be. She had only to reconcile herself to it and its consequences, as well as what it would do to her family.

From her bag she took the letter, filled in the blanks on the back, slipped it into the envelope and sealed it. She needed to ride Mustard into the woods…not in a buggy, but just on a saddle. Walking to the room her brothers shared, she selected a shirt, overalls and a spare hat. Dressing herself that way, she saddled

Mustard and leaped aboard. It was a lot easier at seventeen than it had been at thirteen…longer legs were a help.

Down the trail and toward the Post Office she headed the horse. She mustn't let the aunts see her dressed this way, but the rest of the world didn't matter. She posted the letter and stopped by the Cryer.

Her sister burst into a fit of merriment! She dragged her through the print room to the tiny cafeteria, treating her to coffee and stale donuts. She read the letter soberly and turned to Rowenna. "They're telling you that you are the group leader! Good going, Sis! They couldn't have made a better choice and that's for sure. When I heard you delivered Laverne's babies I wasn't a bit surprised. I've known since you were ten years old that you could do anything you wanted to do. You're going to do a bang up job wherever that is they're sending you to. Anyone who can get that Gold Certificate without even going to the classes can do anything and they'll be lucky to get you."

At the door, she hugged Rowenna and kissed her cheek. Rowenna in her baggy overalls climbed aboard Mustard with thoughts whirling. Jadeen hadn't hugged her since she was three and Jadeen had pulled her out of the room away from her toys. She had never kissed her that Rowenna could remember, and Jadeen hadn't seen a reason why Rowenna didn't jump at the chance to do whatever it was that the Red Cross wanted.

Well, that visit was easy. Next was the woods and the trees. April…and the chinky pins were making their fuzzy balls that turned into burs. Life seemed to be bursting out from every tree and plant, and insects crawled on the rocks. Spring rabbits were everywhere. Black berry vines were loaded with berries. Box turtles were under the vines eating the over-ripes that had fallen. It almost seemed the trees were singing a song of spring. Why couldn't the rest of the world be like Arkansas?

She climbed to the cave. No change. She came down the hill and stopped at Granddad's. He gaped open-mouthed at her baggy attire. She grinned. "What's wrong, Granddad? Jadeen thought it was fun."

"You went to the Cryer office...in that...?"

"I did. It didn't occur to Jadeen that I would turn my country down when they needed me. I think she just can't wait to tell the world that I've gone. You know what else...? She read it like you did. She thought they were telling me gently that I was the group leader." Rowenna shook her head at the sound of the words.

Granddad nodded. Jadeen was no dummy, and she saw the world like it was and she knew what it wanted to hear. "Just don't let the aunts see you like that. We'll have all three of them to bury."

She chuckled, and then turned serious. "I guess you already know. I'm going to accept this or I would always feel like I didn't do what I should have done."

Granddad nodded. He had known. "You'll do fine. When do you go?"

"I have to wait till they tell me. I wonder about the other girls."

She left, and the old man again watched her go. *Thank you, Lord. I seem to see the work of the extra angels. They'll take care of her and she'll be fine. I'll miss her, though.* He turned and went back in his house shaking his own head in disbelief. The fate of many lives was being turned over to a seventeen-year-old girl. Perhaps it was a good thing.

She visited the aunts on the following morning, and spent the rest of the day with Ma and Pa. They tried very hard to be happy for her and save their doubts and tears for later. She left early the next morning. Mustard trip-trapped uneventfully up the hill to the Ridge Road and down.

A few minutes at Laverne's to leave Mustard and hug the babies. Robert Bryce, Mary Rowenna and Anna Jadeen. Anna was just a smidgen smaller, and had likely had to fight for space, but auntie Rowenna had thumped breath into her underdeveloped lungs and she was doing fine. As alike as three peas in a pod. The girls were obviously identical but Bobby was not much different...at this age.

A sisterly hug and she was walking down the street toward the school, the gun making a pleasant weight in her pocket. Gun. GUN! Would they let her keep her gun? Their answer could change things.

Say, Angels...? See if your Boss will let me be like Gideon. If the Boss wants me to go...for sure...then let them agree to the gun. She nodded with approval of her bargain. The Boss should understand that, the way he had helped in the cave and on the Ridge Road. She'd see.

She stepped through the big front door, and her first sight was Dollie wielding a broom. Dollie dropped the broom handle with a crash and grabbed her in a hug. "I didn't think you would be back! I just got out of class and need a cup of tea. Can you come, too?" Pushing the collected dirt in the catcher pan, she led the way to the galley.

Rowenna sketched a quick story about the Red Cross letter with Dollie soberly watching her face. Then, with a sigh, she shared her own concern. "My folks say they can't raise the rest of my fee, and I thought maybe I could take the rest of the course next year. Mrs. Cameron says I wouldn't be permitted to do that because that would be butting into next year's full class, after a space has been held for me this year. It looks like neither of us will be here in the fall."

Rowenna saw the crushed face. Dollie worked so hard and she made top grades. Her memory was fantastic. She must not be forced to drop out. Idea! She doesn't have to!

Here, Rowenna, as a blue cap, had paid no fee. She essentially worked for her keep wherever she could. She still had the reward money from the train robbery. She would see if she could pay Dollie's fee. Dollie mustn't know who did it, but why would that not work? She wished she'd known while she was at home and she would have brought the money.

Hey, Granddad was sure to show up on Friday as usual. He usually carried money. He'd loan it to her.

Miss Osborn, the Scheduler, found them in the galley. "Moffat, Nurse Bennett wants you."

On the gurney was a boy of about ten with a bloody gash all the way down the calf of one leg and he had a torn and bloody sleeve. His face was screwed up in a mass of misery and he refused to cry.

Nurse Bennett handed the scissors to Rowenna. "Barbed wire fence," she explained. "Get the tetanus vaccine out and get it ready. These gashes have rust in them and lockjaw is more of a concern right now than sewing him up. The no-see-em germs that the old folks knew were somewhere, are actually everywhere and especially in rusty nails and barbs. Go ahead and inject, and then help me clean so we can take stitches. He's gashed into the muscle and I want to show you some tricks."

She made quick work of the injection, and then began to wield the scissors on the ripped and bloody sleeve. His morphine shot was taking effect and she could practically see the muscles relaxing. Nurse commented on this. "Tense muscles are more difficult to work with when sewing because they move on their own. This is one good time for morphine. Datura plant used to be used, but the dosage is so inaccurate, it's easy to kill instead of cure. Also, I wanted to tell you something about the tetanus vaccine. Wherever you are...wherever you're sent...always try to have some available. If you need it and don't have it, it's already too late. That particular germ can react with nerves and cause seizures and tightened jaw nerves...also rigid muscles. Then death.

"Moffat, listen to me. Wherever you are that gashes are a danger, insist on the vaccine being available. Sometimes it is omitted from first aid packs. It will be up to you to insist."

Rowenna eased the bloody cloth from under the six-inch gash on the small arm. She looked up into Nurse's eyes. "You know, don't you?"

A nod and a smile. "We'll miss you. But we still have a little while. Maybe as much as a month."

Rowenna jerked at the word. Month! Only a month and there was still so much to learn...like the tetanus vaccine, for instance. "But I..." and no words came past the throat lump.

"No, Moffat. We don't say 'but.' This is what you're cut out to do, and you will be an excellent group leader. You will be there with what is needed when it is needed."

She handed Rowenna the small bulb syringe and the sterile water. "Try to get as much rust out as you can from his arm while I get the thread. We're going to work together on this like the big fancy doctors so! I'll do the leg and you'll do the arm. You will be careful to leave the least scar possible. Boys don't mind scars, but you need the practice."

They worked together mostly in silence, Rowenna pulling up into her memory all the instruction she could. Time to bandage. Oiled paper and the snow-white sterile cloths.

She was to remember these wonderful cloths many times in the next two years. In was on the day of the Red Cross letter that America had declared war on Germany.

The declaration was a necessity not a choice. England was going to fall...without help, and the Red Cross had made a strong bridge between the countries by furnishing volunteers and supplies that would let the American military hit the ground running.

It was today that a loaded supply ship was torpedoed in the channel and sunk with needed medical equipment and hundreds of the folding canvas cots, along with other items too numerous to mention. No personnel were lost, and eventually a few of the other items were saved. It was a tremendous loss.

Granddad still scanned the papers because he could not help himself. Wally was on a ship headed to the channel. The old man was again on his knees before his chair, tears flooding over the work-worn knuckles of his hands. *Not Wally...please Lord. He hasn't even had a chance to do what he volunteered to do.*

Wally, however, had leaped past the suction of the ship sinking into the waters of the channel and had surfaced looking for others. One of the seamen suffered a broken arm. Wally was in the waves again, pulling the man toward him. He wrapped the good arm around his own neck and crawled toward the shore.

Leaving him on solid ground, he swam back through the bubbles of the sinking ship.

All he could collect were a few cushions that arose lazily to the surface. Three of them crammed under one arm and another in his teeth, he crawled through the icy water to the shore. He hauled himself up, creating a bit of needed amusement to bystanders by rescuing seat cushions.

In the midst of the laughter, the explosion of a belated weapon blew the side from the ship. Splintered lumber was working its way up into in a floating surface of chips. Then other things began to rise. The folding cots, with their wooden frames and enough air in the folds of canvas, began to pop through the surface. The incoming tide pushed them closer and closer, until the able bodied began to wade out and haul them in.

One of the little canvas and broomstick aircraft buzzed over, sounding, for all the world, like an Arkansas bumble bee. The pilot peered down, circled the damage once more and zoomed off.

In a couple of hours a lorry appeared, followed by two more. The humans and the cots were loaded aboard. The location was marked on the map because when the tide left the channel, the shore would be strewn with many other items, many still usable.

England had reached the point of being unable to afford to waste even one thing.

NATHAN WILKINSON, CAPTAIN, MEDICAL CORPS

Nathan didn't even have an address. Here he was at some fenced in location where men from all parts of the country were congregated. He was informed that when his designated ocean-going transportation arrived and was unloaded…was checked over and repacked…he would be on his way. To somewhere.

Meanwhile, he was being introduced to the intricacies of the automobile. Important thing for him to know, he was told. He was schooled on the safest method of driving and what not to do. He was given practice at the wheel, and hours at looking under the bonnet...sometimes called a hood. He was schooled in the emergency repair of the rubber tubes that fit inside the hard-rubber casings enclosing the wheels.

Nathan had always intended to check out the gasoline powered auto, but it had not yet become important in Wishbone. Too many time-consuming repairs to be done, and he would attend to having an auto after some of the "bugs" had been engineered out of the machine. But that was not to be...and Wishbone was far away.

He and many others were being so rapidly immersed into the innards of the auto that their heads swam. On April 10, being hardly four days into the war on Germany, Nathan and a number of others were aboard the ship plunging its way through the Atlantic.

Back in Eureka Springs, Rowenna had finally settled her head to what she was always going to do. The aim, now, was to accumulate as much information as possible in the time remaining. Creeping into her thoughts were the twelve other girls who were, without doubt, in her same situation. Beset with wonderings...waitings...fears...and exhausted from trying to imagine their immediate future.

Granddad could, indeed, forward Rowenna the huge amount of $25.00. He had planned on doing a bit of shopping while in the bigger city, but it was nothing that would not wait.

Rowenna slipped the money into Mrs. Cameron's hand and begged to be anonymous. "Could you say someone in the town who knew about the school, wanted to give a gift to some student who could use it? If she knew it was from me, it would spoil our friendship."

Mrs. Cameron nodded, agreeably. What she actually told Student Nurse Duffy was, "Duffy, step in the office as I have something to tell you."

Then, "The school has received a donation of considerable size, and we have decided its best use would be to use it against your second semester. That would get you to completion and we think it would be well used there. I tell you now, so you won't be concerned and just work on your lessons…. Everything is paid for."

With wide happy eyes, Dollie reached for the older woman's hand and squeezed it in both of hers. "Oh, thank you…thank you! It was so good of you to consider me, and I will do my best to make it worthwhile."

"My dear, of course you will do your best. That is why this gift is in the best place it could be."

Dollie couldn't wait to excitedly confide in Rowenna. "I think I know what you mean about angels! I think one must have been watching out for me. If I just knew who gave the gift, I would love to thank them."

Rowenna found it easy to be happy with her. "Miss Dollie… if the person who gave the gift wanted you to know who he or she was, you would have been told. So just remember that!"

Dollie's huge, dark eyes stared into her friend's eyes as though she would like to look into her very soul. "I will. And no one has any idea of how hard it was for me to get here and how much this means to me."

Rowenna looked back for a silent minute. "I'm not sure about that. There's likely someone who knows."

"The angels…?"

Rowenna nodded. "Yes, them as well."

Dollie drew in a deep breath and let out. Then she silently decided to let the matter fall. Rowenna seemed to know something, and it was likely something that Dollie, herself, did not want to know.

Nathan's orders stated that he was in command of the "cadre" that would be operating Somme River Medical Detachment. His cadre consisted of ten men headed by the three officers, himself as captain and two lieutenants. These three would head up the operation with others added when available. Each of the officers had two assistants…one sergeant and one corporal. The tenth man was the Signal Corp with two assistants to be named. Others would be added gradually, as that seemed the better plan.

Somme River MedDet would, at first, be stationed in a fortress in the south of England for further intense training. The British and French armies were joined in the attempt to free the mouth of the Somme River so they could regulate traffic, and there was to be an additional bloody encounter at the Ypres Salient to create a place for the Navy to settle its nurse corps. The Ypres (I-per) River was in truth a natural canal draining a large portion of the lowest part of Belgium.

The French word "Salient" referred to a slight rise of the topography in a pointed shape. This particular salient projected out into the channel near the Dover cliffs of England. It was an extremely valuable piece of land for its ability furnish a good visual of the area, and also because of it, along with Dunkirk, being the closest point of land to England.

In Emperor Wilhelm's "great rush to the sea" he was phenomenally successful in the first rush, but the British and French massed forces and won it back in a couple of weeks. By then, the German Albatross had perfected its shooting range and airtime between refueling, and Germany struggled, trench by trench, to take it back.

In early spring of 1917, the French reinforcements came in from the south and established a foothold between the Ypres River and the Somme River, approximately seventy-five miles apart.

The whole of Belgium consisted of sections of land between the network of canals that connected to eventually flow into the Iper River, that the activity reminded an English captain that the army appeared to him like bugs scurrying when a rock was moved. He named the activity of his army to be a "bug out." It differed from an advancement or retreat as the "bugs" were not looking for a certain place to go as much as a place to "not be." It created confusion rather than a plan.

It was others, later on, that gave credit to the Ypres Salient as being the origin of the military "bug out," and who was there to argue?

The, also important, mouth of the Somme River was won and retained with a great loss of personnel, but it gave an important access inland that could aid in the eventual defense of Paris.

The thoughts of the planners were that the river mouth must be retained at all cost, though the casualties would be high. The sooner they could establish a medical detachment and an availability of ambulance service at the mouth, the quicker progress could be made inward to Luxemburg and further north. But that would be later.

The area where Nathan and his cadre were being held pending the deployment was a hastily put together structure built onto what was originally a stable where the English "lord of the manor" had kept his horses. The manor house was now empty of its human occupants, and the blue-blooded equine stock long ago conscripted by the military.

Nathan's detachment of ten men attended lectures and exercises on evasive actions and anything the officers could think of that would keep the men alive and retain the spot of land in allied hands.

Overhead was a frequent buzz of the experimental aircraft that rolled off the factory line. Minor adjustments here and a slant of the wing there, and the "test pilot" could assess the difference in its handling…better or worse.

Also overhead was the training activity of new pilots. Strong sons of local farmers were interspersed with the recruits from the American Midwest. There were the three Fire Eagle brothers who eventually made their place in history. Those young men from the plains seemed to be akin to their namesake birds. They were obviously meant to fly and fly they did.

There was Raymond Tall Tree who lost his plane behind German lines. It took a month of hiding and night-marching to get himself back to the salient and demand to be taken across the channel. By now he was "good and mad" and "someone would pay" for bringing him down out of the sky and destroying his "wings." He hopped aboard the supply launch to Dover and his "outfit." A week later he was again dodging the Albatross squadrons to "observe and report" on enemy positions.

Raincrow was another pilot who made his mark in the skies, flying up from a point on the Seine called Rouen. Now John Wallace Hopkins was tossed among them, along with Jimmy Simmons and Darrel Mackinzie. While Nathan watched the instructor's pointer indicate the best route up the Somme River, some of the overhead buzz was created by his former neighbor, Wally, concentrating on his "steering" and trying to remember everything he was told just last week.

Nathan's instructor said that "whenever possible" he should begin the journey up river with the wounded when the Atlantic tide came in, giving the barges a strong lift up-river before the motor launch was forced to use precious petrol. By the same token, returning the barges should be scheduled with the outgoing tide so that greater strings of barges could be controlled by one motor launch. It was highly difficult to stock petrol in place in these newly won areas, so that made the fuel a commodity almost as valuable as ammo and food.

Wally, buzzing over the building where Nathan attended classes, might never know of the existence of a building below, as it was located in a tree-studded green field totally camouflaged with the green, brown and gold net over all roofs, and all vehicles were kept undercover.

Camouflage was extremely important. Even now, slats of wood made into panels covered with canvas, were being off-loaded with the tide onto the muddy mouth of the river Somme. These were hammered together into something called a barrack that would sleep about two dozen men, and it held cots and stretchers for twice that many wounded. Pre-made shelves were clicked together, and metal panels were in place on the bare ground for purposes of furnishing the medical personnel a place to stand that was more or less possible to keep reasonably clean. Better facilities were promised. When possible.

Due to the lowness of the land, the underground water table was high, and a portable drill created a source of water that was hoped to be "clean." Water at the mouth of the river would be next to impossible to make sanitary enough to use. The French river, having run through too many battles with too many injured and too many dead horses, was a breeding place for germs. The Somme River could be counted on as a ferry for the barges… essentially nothing more.

Nathan practiced "putting his fear on hold" as he was scheduled to be the "go to" person in his group. How…pray tell… could anything like this happen? Good, old, easy-going Nathan from Arkansas being in charge of a medical detachment…? When all he wanted was a small medical supply business. It would have been the stuff of nightmares if he had not been so weary by nightfall that dreamless sleeping was no problem.

It was decided by someone…no one ever knew just who… that the cadre of ten would be the vanguard of the entire program. Captain Nathan Wilkinson, medic, Lieutenant Brady Marshall, animal handler and Mitchell Meyers, ambulance handler.

The signalman, Lieutenant John Foster, was a very important addition to the cadre. The Morse code, as well as other codes, were transmitted by a variety of methods invented during the last three or four decades, but the radio/telephone (using pioneer wireless transmission) had its first and most extensive use on and over the English Channel. There were ship to shore transmissions, and some wireless communication from Dover, England mostly to the Iper Salient (Belgium) in late 1917 and early 1918. Improvements were fastly coming about as the need became greater. While the army pushed farther into Europe more distance was added to the ability, as well as interception ability of the German systems.

Lt. Foster was the perfect choice for one who could "work the bugs out of a system," and found himself with twenty-four-hour duty. He was instrumental in passing information to other stations in Belgium, and his electronic ability stood him in good stead.

These ten men, officers and enlisted together, had spent the whole of the ocean voyage getting acquainted and accessing the abilities and strengths of each other, as their very lives would quite well depend on that knowledge.

There would be many more personnel added to the Somme River Medical Detachment, but it was decided that additions should be gradual. Tossing too many "strangers" together until a system was set up could create confusion.

And confusion was something they truly did not need. It was about this time that the acronym "SNAFU" was born. Broken apart, the letters meant, "Situation normal. All fouled up!"

FROM THE NOTES OF CAPTAIN MARLENE CRAVENS

It might be well to note that many conferences between high level personnel of different activities were of minimal importance, but Captain Marlene Cravens, RN, felt that it was necessary for this one to be documented for future references and perhaps training purposes.

This particular officer had been chosen to be escort and advisor of Alpha One, the introduction of American nurses into the battlefield region. This was likely because of her own home region being near to that of her assignment. She would accompany (some said "chaperone" but that was not accurate) a group of young nurses to a location in the English Channel where a hospital ship would serve the wounded in northern France and Belgium. This group was to be called Alpha One, hoping there would eventually be a "Two" and a "Three."

These young ladies, all fully certified, would tend to the first aid and the daily care of the war wounded until they could return to battle, be moved to a field hospital or be repatriated to America.

It was goal of the experiment to move the detachment ashore as soon as a safe place could be won from the enemy. This would put help much closer to those who needed help. Alpha One would consist of:

Rowenna Moffat, Group Leader with Gold Certification.
Katie Campbell
Carol Gian
Laura Carpenter
Ollie Kettle
Rosie Coyote
Barbara Reeves
Helen DuPrey
Twila Screaming Eagle
Gertrude Ezell
Susan Spotted Pony
Fannie Gretna
Evelyn Walker

The high-level conferences consisted of General Daniel McGuffy, US Navy who would be in charge of the transfer and the hosting until a spot of land could be "cleared."

And Major Isabelle Griswold, American Red Cross, Regional commander of the American Midwest Region.

Captain Marlene Cravens, RN Escort and adviser, Alpha One.

THIS CONVERSATION TOOK PLACE 20 MAY 1917

GENERAL: "I understand all thirteen of the young women are less than twenty years old. Is this wise?"

MAJOR: "They are seventeen to nineteen, and they all struggled to get this education, it was their choice of what to do with their life, and, most importantly, they were the only ones who agreed to be assigned. We considered it to be wise to accept these young ladies, as they were who was interested in our experiment." (A faint note of sarcasm tinged her voice.)

GENERAL: "There were no volunteers in their mid-twenties?"

MAJOR: "Sir, that would have been our first choice, but by that age, the ladies would be married and therefore unavailable, even if they choose to leave their families and risk their lives. Girls with nursing certificates are snapped up quicker than a duck on a June bug." (The General ignored the comparison.)

GENERAL: "What provisions have been made for their safety?"

MAJOR: "While on the ship, they are as safe as the soldiers. On land we will do our best. We will be in contact with them at all times, and their provisions will be provided by motor launch or airdrop. Captain Cravens will be the 'on site' supervisor."

CAPTAIN: "Sir, I will be with them for the first two weeks at least. After that, I may be away for two or three days at a time in an emergency situation. Three male personnel will be assigned to the location when they move on shore. They will be a medic and two orderlies. Others will be available to be assigned as needed."

GENERAL: "It is difficult for me to imagine young ladies of this age as being able to govern themselves, let alone perform such an important duty."

CAPTAIN: "Sir, with all due respect, these nurses were hand-picked by an experienced psychologist for their particular skills and abilities.

"The group leader, Miss Moffat, is a sharpshooter with her hand gun. She has interrupted a kidnapping and protected two persons, saved her own life when her buggy and horse were accosted by a robber. She has nursed two persons through the measles, alone, and she delivered triplet babies for her sister. These actions are listed among other accomplishments.

"Miss Campbell is the oldest of her siblings and rescued them from the second floor of a burning building. She has knowledge of plants that are suitable for food, has experience in sewing clothing for younger sister.

"Miss Carpenter, as well as others, is group oriented. Her ability with a gun is remarkable, considering she had never picked one up. She seems fearless in activities, and swims well.

"Miss Coyote has skill in running, also in weaving which indicates excellent hand skill. She, along with others, swims well. She is a storyteller which will help to entertain her co-workers, and that is important. I might add, she is skilled with the bow and arrow should we decide to assign her one." (The General struggled to hide an amused smile.)

"Several of the girls enjoy cooking and are inventive with new foods. All passed the swimming exercise. Three of them are conversant in French, and two can speak their native language of Kiowa. Some show skill in leadership ability and others in following instructions. Without exception, they desired and fought for their education and I am amazed that they actually volunteered.

"Miss Spotted Pony and Miss Moffat tested with Olympic skill in swimming and diving. Miss Spotted Pony also plays the flute and has won ribbons for her ability to throw a hatchet accurately, should that skill be required. She is quick to attempt what she has never tried before.

"I could go on and on, Sir, because I have spent the last month with these young ladies, and they really want to weld themselves into a group, and during that that month, they sorted themselves out and into their own special niches. Would that possibly answer your question?"

GENERAL: "Most ably, Captain. I am fascinated by the colorful names. Will that be a problem in any way?"

CAPTAIN: "I can't see how it would, Sir. Those names were set long before these young ladies were born and were certainly designated by either English or French settlers or trappers. We know that English was not spoken by their ancestors, so the colorful names such as Spotted Pony, could be a trapper's attempt to Anglicize the native word of the same meaning. Certainly 'Spotted' or 'Pony' (instead of horse) were not in the native language, but this way lets them keep the meaning of their heritage."

MAJOR: "Sir, is there any other information you need?"

GENERAL: "This seems to be complete. We can go forward with this experiment with the US Navy being temporary host. You may proceed as soon as convenient."

MAJOR: "Thank you, Sir. We are currently preparing the railway chits to pay their passage to the coast."

Meeting adjourned.

Captain Cravens had a lot to think about. In her thirty-one years of age there had been a lot of "firsts" since she had joined the Red Cross. There were times she had mulled over her decision…and it certainly wasn't for the money. It wasn't really for "patriotism" either, though that had grown and was what kept her in place now.

The experiment with the younger, newly certified, nurses was certainly interesting. She had brought her Alpha One young ladies (girls?) to the Central Hotel in Fayetteville to get acquainted, hoping that if there was a "ringer" in the group it would show. If someone proved to be pampered, physically frail, unduly fearful or even one who just changed her mind and wanted to turn back, it would be found now so she could bring on an alternate.

The twelve plus a group leader was a number that seemed sufficient to include the needed traits and talents to work together…alone. And the four weeks she had spent with them gave her no reason to doubt the choices that had been made for her.

Very interesting was the group leader. Though being one of the younger in the group, the difference between seventeen and nineteen is not great, and this particular girl seemed extraordinarily solid. Miss Moffat was a natural at leading by example and was so approachable that others wanted to join her. She was what some would refer to as being everyday-ordinary and easy to get along with.

It would remain to be seen how she would do with decisions, though Captain Cravens saw no one better, and when Katie Campbell and Susan Spotted Pony "took to her" so readily, the others fell in.

None of these girls were pushed in this direction against their will, each had worked hard for good scores, and there were family wishes to hold them back from volunteering but they had not wavered. Now they would be sent home for three weeks for their "goodbyes" and she'd see if they all showed up for the train to take them to the Washington, D. C. Headquarters…and then to the Mercy Ship headed for England.

LAST DAYS AT HOME IN WISHBONE

Rowenna was puzzled at the faint aura of dread she felt as she stepped from the Frisco Mail Train into the Wishbone Depot. There was the tiny thread of dread (fear? guilt? regret?) that wound itself around her thoughts.

"Granddad, I wonder if I made a mistake and just thought my angel was telling me what her Boss said. I'm just seventeen and I've only had less than a year of experience. Surely there's been a mistake."

Granddad, who had met her at the depot, now sat with her in the diner at the tiny table. She was so close she could see every wrinkle on his face and study every flicker of his expression. She saw his head of snow-white hair nod agreeably…maybe like she had just said "the weather looked like it might rain." Could she pull some sort of encouragement from that?

Granddad sipped his coffee and set the mug on the table. "I understand what you mean about the mistake. That's exactly what Gideon said, remember? After that, God made it perfectly clear that he meant what he said. Of course, it took the actual sight of an angel for Gideon to believe, and it seems you were convinced just by receiving help and listening to your thoughts. Perhaps you didn't need an angel."

"But…Granddad…? I'm only sev…."

"Seventeen? That's about the age of David when he slew the giant, and the age of Joseph when he was sold into Egypt to make a way to save his family from the coming famine. You're about ten years older than Samuel when he was called. I don't think God cares about the ages of the humans he needs."

"But if I can't take my gun, that will be like Gideon's fleece.** I haven't heard about it, and I only have three weeks to hear. Maybe I don't have to go."

It was then that Granddad took from his pocket a handful of letters. One was addressed to her. It was unopened, though Granddad must have been very curious, not knowing why she had directed her letter with his address.

Slowly and deliberately, she lifted the flap and read:

Our best greetings to you, Miss Moffat:

As regards your request to bring your personal firearm with you, we feel we must advise you of certain rules made for the safety and economy of the Alpha Project.

We regret we might have a rule that you might not prefer to live with, but we will attempt to explain our action. It is certainly acceptable for you to have your weapon with you until you reach Red Cross Headquarters, and then it must be returned to your family with the clothes you wore on the trip. At that time, your personal safety becomes the responsibility of the Red Cross.

Along with your issue of clothing there will be a 9mm Walther handgun that has been chosen for its reliability and is of a weight and design which seemed to fit in feminine hands more comfortably than some other choices.

For uniformity of ammunition and ease of handling it was decided that all weapons, and consequently all ammunition, should be uniform and thus interchangeable. We hope this will not be a problem with you and we appreciate that you have a skill and ability that will, without doubt, easily transfer to this more powerful weapon.

In closing, we might take this opportunity to express our appreciation for your offer of service, which we are certain was not in your original life plan. It is thought that you and others like you will make a success of the Alpha Project and be of great service to your country and an important aid to the young men in the trenches.

Your American Red Cross.

Rowenna handed the letter to Granddad. She was too close to tears to risk reading it to him. What...really, what...? could answer her question more clearly? It was somewhat like when Gideon asked God for the fleece to be wet and the grass dry... and God made the fleece so wet Gideon wrung a bowl of water from it. It was like saying "I meant exactly what I said and did not make a mistake."

Granddad read slowly and thoughtfully and handed it back with a sly smile as though he was not at all surprised. Rowenna would never know how hard it had been for him to smile when every fiber within his being, now begged for her to have been turned down. For her to have be released from her promise. *Why, Lord...?*

How could the powerful cannons and the trained young men need a seventeen-year-old girl who weighed barely 110 pounds? But then, how did King Saul need a boy with a sling and a stone when he had an army of skilled soldiers at his side? It was all in how you looked at it, and how well you were in tune with God's plan.

Rowenna stopped in to see the great aunts. All talking at once, they explained the care they had taken with new under things for her "trip." They presented her with a box containing six pairs of drawers and six camisoles made from the softest of delicate fabric and trimmed in hand-tatted Irish lace. The camisole straps were made of a tatted band of lace interwoven with a matching pink satin ribbon.

Rowenna tried to hide her tears, but failed. The aunts rushed to her comfort. "Oh, honey! It'd be least we could do. We wouldn't want you to start out with old under things."

And, "Now, dear, when you see what kind of pettislip you need, you let us know and we'll send you some."

She kissed and hugged them all and sought for an acceptable answer. "I won't get to have my holster pettislip. They make all of us wear the same thing, and they furnish it. My new gun will be a different shape."

Eyes wide with horror. "You can't have your gun? Are you sure...?"

"Oh, yes, I'm sure. But they're going to give me a better one that will be just like what the other nurses have. I get to leave mine own here so I'll have it when I come back home."

Somewhat mollified, they nodded. That made sense... somehow. At least as much sense as anything else did, anymore. Getting old was so confusing. Seldom did they agree. It was a rare thing that the three ladies had decided to totally agree with each other.

Rowenna climbed the hill to her childhood home, feeling even more alienated from her childhood. The familiar rocks and shrubs seemed to be part of a dream she had years ago. The mental picture of the under things in the box she carried produced a wry smile. They were exactly something a girl would put in her marriage chest...clearly indicating that the wonderful aunts had no idea of what she had agreed to do.

By the time she reached the house, she had decided to make a present of the under things to Jadeen who could use them very well. The aunts would be horrified at what Rowenna was actually going to be issued.

The military nurses' issue of clothing was made from course fabric in a one-size-fits-all pattern...with firm, no-nonsense elastic...light tan color and no trimming. The fabric was supposed to dry quickly from being washed. That was for summer.

The winter under things were made from something almost like canvas with leggings extending below the knees. The thick fabric was presumed to be warmer, and the extra length would an advantage in a damp climate near the North Sea. There was one reprieve...the lighter weight summer wear could be worn under the winter wear for extra warmth (and possibly comfort) if desired.

It was no particular accident that the young ladies of Alpha One were of a similar size. All clothing was designed for interchangeability within the group. Keeping thirteen sets of clothing separate was an unneeded chore, they would soon agree. By the same token the linen/wool blend of the dresses did not wrinkly badly. Gone were the blouses with a separate fitted skirt. They would hardly have time for the flatiron to keep them crisp.

An extremely important clothing item was the coverall apron constructed almost like a sleeveless dress, semi-full skirted and open-backed. These shell garments would save the laundering of the uniform dress and were more easily washed…dried readily… and could be quickly changed.

Also needed in the marshy low country were the gum boots. They came in small and medium, very little difference in the sizes making them almost a one-size-fits-all as well. Handkerchiefs were squares of olive green cotton as were the machine-knitted stockings.

Work uniforms included a kerchief for enclosing hair rather than the attractive white hat. That one item caused a momentary dismay, but their good sense told them that starched, white hats in the field would only be a nuisance.

The winter camisoles were more like undershirts and constructed from the linsey/woolsy fabric to create warmth. They had the pettislips attached as a skirt, and Captain Cravens had explained, with a chuckle, that there might be times when they would decide to wear more than one of these garments under their uniform dresses. For additional warmth.

Finally, there were loose fitting short jackets and long wool capes for the outdoors. These could be worn individually or together as the weather dictated. Oil-treated canvas hooded capes were issued for the rainy season.

Another wry smile from Rowenna and a sigh. If the aunts only saw what she would be wearing, they might just pass out from the indignity of it all and demand that the Red Cross change these rules…immediately!

Ma and Pa had tried to be accepting of this unimaginable thing that was to happen to their thirteenth kid. There was the eleventh kid who headed for the stage, and the twelfth on her way to running the Wishbone Cryer. It was likely a good thing they stopped at thirteen, as the next one might just decide to take over the government!

Their intention was to survive this goodbye period and to pretend that absolutely nothing had changed, and life was securely on track. They could pretend that Rowenna would bide her time until the right young man appeared. That she would develop an interest in her marriage chest that contained only a few items and all of them gifts from family. They acted as though she was just another daughter to be pulled through her seventeenth year and not one that would be halfway around the world before the autumn leaves dropped.

She reached the hilltop house with a sigh.

Ma was out in the back yard plucking the feathers from a large Dominicker rooster and stuffing the softer breast feathers into a cheese cloth bag so they would dry properly. They would be used as needed for pillows, comforter quilts and mattress pads. Ma told her "no thanks" that she could finish this little job and they'd cut the chicken in pieces for frying as he was still young and tender.

Pa waved a greeting, stepped into the wagon and clicked to the team of mules. The meadow hay was dry and now must be brought to the hay barn. Just another normal day at home on the farm, and Rowenna felt as though it had nothing to do with her. She fought for way to seem normal in it.

"Ma...I'll change and go help Pa with the hay."

"No, dear. You needn't do that."

"But I want to, Ma. And I can move the team to the next pile. We'll be through sooner."

Ma looked her, one hand holding the legs of the half-naked rooster and the other with a handful of fluffy breast feathers...the breeze coming up the mountain picking off one...then another... of the feathers and carrying they away. Silently she nodded and

145

turned and watched until Rowenna's rushing feet took her to the kitchen door to change her shoes.

Pa slowed the mules down to a mosey…there was a chance his thirteenth kid would come with him…this one last time.

She did.

*Judges, chapter 6, specifically verse 15
**Judges, chapter 6, verses 36 to 40.

THE RECAPTURE OF THE YPRES SALIENT

(The Iper Promontory/Bluff)

The command had originated with the English high power and signed of all the way down to the generals who parceled out the orders…to the captains and over to the boots on the ground. The sergeants would make it work.

The Ypres (Iper) River and, secondly, the Somme River must be won back and held or all else would be lost. The German army under generals such as Otto von Bismarck had succeeded twice in actually stepping into the English Channel separating Europe from England.

Twice the fledgling allies had fought them back, and now they had received a wonderful surge from Australia. The Australian Force was well-fed and fresh and was currently landing on the low bluff that extended into the channel and was about twenty miles over the water to Britain.

In their "great rush to the sea" OttoVon Bismarck's army had not destroyed everything in their path, as they had been instructed to do. An army cannot forge ahead and stop to burn farms at the same time, so the Tancrez Farm near the bluff had survived. How could it have been missed, the historians later questioned, as the farm was extensive with three large and well-built structures.

The Australians offloaded onto motor launches and plowed their way up-current to the trenches of the English army. The Iper River was, in fact, natural system of drainage canals creating in a web through western Belgium. Each of its tributaries was a battle

146

ground in itself, though not a large one, and the southern army filled in as the fatigued English riflemen retreated for a breath and a re-group....

The Battalion medic had patched up the bleeding as best he could, and the fond hope was that the injured be transferred to the barges and sent back to the channel hospital ship. So time consuming and unwieldy. There would be losses even as they were being moved down stream. There had been no choice. If healthy fighters had to be assigned to the wounded, who would hold the hard-won ground?

As the weary Britts moved back, they could hear the buzz overhead as the observation aircraft were reporting on troop positions. The weary men watched with a ray of encouragement. It seemed the air force was actually getting planes across the channel and back with needed information.

The Scout Aircraft, SA3, dipped as low as was safe so the observer could note, best as he could with the small aircraft being tossed about, where the battle lines were at this moment. The observer noted with excitement that the barges were returning full which meant the fresh Australians troops were now in charge.

The observer also noted that the Tancrez Farm had not yet been touched, and that would make the generals happy. What's more, he saw the huge Red Cross insignia. It was painted in scarlet, actually more like blood red, and was attached to the ground facing upward as had been commanded. It was important to continuously observe the farm to make sure it was still in Red Cross hands.

The tiny plane dipped and turned, conserving precious air time, but still had eight miles to go before returning to England. While the pilot fought the errant air currents with an eye on his compass, the observer noted the activity at the mouth of the Somme River, and that there were no enemy troops within sight. The Somme River was just as important as the Iper River but was much more easily protected.

The little SA 3 turned out of the headwind and rode its force back to the base. The Scout Aircraft facility could turn out a plane every hour, but they were still of the low-powered, wooden and canvas construction. Engineers worked feverously to trim weight and reduce air friction while increasing power but were still far behind the German Fokker and the Albatross. The light planes were wonderful for observation, but a war could not be won with only observers.

Changes were being made so rapidly that no one bothered to name the configurations, deciding just to number them and keep working. Across the island another factory was working toward a metal-encased, sleek design that would be called the Spitfire. It was far from ready and would not be of use in this war...its own war would be waged about a decade later.

Wally had gazed with wonder at the tiny Scout Aircraft. He could feel a tingle in his hands, likely the same as David as he picked up the five smooth stones for his sling.* Sort of a "with help, I can take this on." He had a background for this aerial contraption, rather like David had used the sling while protecting his sheep. Wally had faced down the combustion engine in the automobile and won. How could this be different?

While still a member of the Royal Flying Corps, he listened to the instructions, squirming in his seat to get his hands on the steering stick. When he was actually allowed to sit in the pilot's seat, his request of the higher power was "angel, this is terribly important. You were assigned to me and I'm certain I can count on you to ride along and guide my hands."

The first exercises were simple. He was to point the nose upward, clear the wheels from the ground, count to ten and lower, gently, back to the ground. John Wallace Hopkins had been taught to obey and to take instructions, but he had to mentally force his hands to bring him back to the practice field after the count of ten. He felt his fingers tingle from the force of his grip. He wanted to go on...and on...and ON...!!

The wheels touched the soil of the English practice field and he rolled to a stop. His instructor was beside him. "Hopkins, go back up and circle left into the wind. Come down on a count on twenty."

Wally nodded, telling himself, *Be still, my fluttering heart!* He followed a series of commands until his training period was over. It was with a crushing reluctance he relinquished his seat to the next trainee.

There were more classroom exercises, but Wally could hardly concentrate. Richard Blue Thunder sat beside him, just about as nervous. The American had "R Blue" on his uniform. Two names seemed enough to trainee Blue, but "Thunder" better matched his actions. Together they sat, the Americans both nervously anxious to climb into the skies and transport these magic toys across the island so they could be used by the struggling English army.

Two weeks later the two volunteers from the American Midwest sat, each in his own cockpit, as their propellers were whirled by expert hands, revving up the guts of the small noisy engine.

One after another they arose in single formation, 2nd Lt. Blue not yet at the peak of his climb when 2nd Lt. Hopkins was waved on. There were twenty of the small crafts to follow. This went on day after day. The flyers were to write down any small suggestion they had on the handling and thoroughly express any fear they experienced.

They could not afford to lose pilots…and possibly more than that, they must not lose the aircraft! England was becoming desperate. There was, however, a sunrise on the eastern horizon.

America had finally joined the war!

*I Samuel 17:40

JADEEN'S SENDOFFS

Jadeen knew her responsibility when she saw it. It was entirely up to her to inform the world that the little Arkansas town of Wishbone was doing its part in the war effort.

At first she had considered a tremendous write up covering their three offerings…Nathan, Wally and Rowenna. Then, after her good sense kicked in, she knew it would be much better to give each of their people their own edition and thereby she could spread her talented write-ups over almost an entire month. Nathan first.

WISHBONE CRYER, NEWS FROM THE WAR

We're still hearing good things from our fellows who have volunteered to help the Britts. Nathan Wilkinson is now a captain and is preparing to make his name known on the mainland of Europe.

With the arrival of troops from Australia, the Somme River has become available to create a medical detachment at the river's mouth to receive the casualties to be returned to England. He will be responsible to bring wounded for first aid treatment.

In addition, the ambulance detail will be used when roadways are cleared. There will be times that food supplies will by moved forward in these automobiles, most of which were donated by householders fleeing the army.

Captain Nathan Wilkinson will act as medical officer for the detachment, binding wounds, setting bones and outfitting with splints and crutches as needed.

The above details were gleaned from letter to his family, and from reports from the front. Like his parents, we miss him every day when we think he should be at the Market filling us in on community happenings.

The truth is, though, in a war there are sacrifices to be made by all, and those we make here are nothing to what our hometown son is going through. We send him our best wishes until we see him again.

Jadeen Moffat re-read her write-up and adjusted a word here and there. She would like to have made it much longer, but she had learned that people only read as long as their interest was

piqued, and no longer. Sometimes it seemed that less was more...
fewer words better than too many. There would be other things to
add later. There was always a tomorrow.

A week later she put together all she could gather on her
cousin, Wally. Never close as friends, she had always admired him
for the way he actively attached his attention to whatever he did,
whether he liked it or not. When Wally had a job (or a lesson)
to do, he did not veer away until it was done. He might try to
avoid what he didn't like, but when the chips were down, he got
it done.

The family did not get a lot of letters, and that surprised no
one, but when the few they got were pieced together Jadeen was
sure she had enough details to interest her readers.

WISHBONE CRYER, NEWS FROM THE WAR

As many of you already know, our hometown boy,
Wally Hopkins, has now been picked off from the Red
Cross and added to the Royal Flying Corps. He was
recruited to assist the ferrying of the new aircraft from
the factory to the coast of England, and they could not
have made a better choice.

Those who know Wally know that he always does a
good job. Most of you remember how evenly he placed
the letters of the slogans onto the church marquee! So
now he's placing airplanes on another side of the British
Islands! Good going, Cousin Wally!

Another bit of information is that he had been teamed
up with another American, Richard Blue Thunder,
from over west of Tulsa, Oklahoma. They seem to have
hit it off well, and I hear they will be flying observation
planes over the channel to Belgium. We hope they
are good at dodging anti-aircraft fire. We've heard of
some of the observation planes being brought down by
German guns, but we know if anyone can survive, it'll
be Wally.

Wally never did anything halfway, and it's likely the other fellow is the same. Arkansas and Oklahoma produce the best, and the military is fortunate for volunteers like Wally and we here at home know that his guardian angel has been commissioned to take charge and keep him safe.

There'll be more later. Keep in touch for this column.

Jadeen nodded to herself after reading again that last sentence. It was clearly written for Granddad Hopkins who was taking the war very hard. And here was The Girl With the Gun, poised for her own flight into the war. Granddad will be devastated. He thinks that girl raises his sun in the mornings. Maybe she does.

Anyway, she'd wait until her sister actually left the American shore to write the first piece, and then she could write another one later when she arrived. Rowenna would be sure to write to Granddad and Ma and Pa, so she'd have a lot of material.

On the other hand, she could write a small update now that she had gone through her orientation and was…for certain… going.

WISHBONE CRYER, UPDATE ON THE GIRL WITH THE GUN

Our hometown girl came through her orientation with flying colors as we knew she would. She is currently on her "goodbye" leave, and will be leaving as group leader with a total of thirteen young ladies from seventeen to twenty. It's interesting to note that the group is composed of thirteen. It matches the thirteenth kid, somehow.

But as was we are reminded, Joshua circled Jericho thirteen times (once a day for six days and seven times on the seventh day) so as Rev. Irvin Hopkins pointed out, "luck" depends on who's side you're on. Joshua didn't lose a man in that fight.

We're going to miss her, and no creature more than Granddad Hopkin's yellow horse, Mustard. I hear the poor fellow is long-faced and grieving already.

I'll keep you updated on our girl. Keep watching this column.

Jadeen smiled at her own cleverness. Rowenna was such good copy, and here she had assigned herself at least three columns in the next month! *Good going, Jadeen!*

Not only that...a wonderful idea had lodged itself in Jadeen's fertile brain. She knew, for a fact, that her sister felt naked and unprepared when she did not have her gun, and that she did not trust the mail service to get it back to Wishbone where it belonged.

Jadeen sighed with pleasure over her new idea. If she offered to go with Rowenna when she had to report to Fayetteville, then Rowenna could have her gun along, and Jadeen could bring it home.

Not only that, when she got to Fayetteville and delivered Rowenna to the Red Cross, she could be picked up by one of her sisters who lived in Fayetteville and make a party of the trip. If she did that, there is no end to the wonders she might see and be able to report on.

Also, just being trusted to bring back the famous gun would raise her status in Wishbone. If she expected to get promotions, then her importance must be foremost in her efforts.

And while she considered all of this, she sat in her copywriter's chair feeling cool and comfortable in the deliciously soft under things made by the aunts. It was a fabulous gift, but not one she could mention. A note in the classified that she had wonderful new under wear would not help her at all, but the trusted transport of the gun would.

Of course, the aunts would gladly have created the same gift for her if she just spent the time with them as Rowenna had, but she was so busy at the Cryer. At least, that's what she told herself.

And Granddad had read Jadeen's articles and updates with interest, as he always did. Then he stared out the window practically into the long golden face of Mustard. So helpless to make a change, the animal just waited…and watched. Like his owner.

No! Granddad drew back from the window, put on his hat and walked to Main Street. Just off Main was the bookstore. If they didn't have what he wanted, he'd have them order it. He was cheered slightly by the burst of energy to do something… anything.

He had always frequented the bookstore, so the manager tended to ignore him unless he needed help…which was rare. This time was no different.

There, in the genuine leather black cover with the whisper-light tissue pages was the book. New Testament and Psalms. Slim and trim with a tidy zipper to close it in.

He picked up three of the books and paid for them. The manager did not bother to ask what they were for, as the whole town knew what the old preacher was going through. Apparently the old man had added Nathan to his grandchildren. He, like the whole town, missed Nathan's face in the store.

He had acquired addresses for the fellows, just in case he needed them. And now he did. A strange address of APO, England, plus Nathan's serial number seemed to be enough to insure it being delivered. John Wallace Hopkins was attached to the Royal Flying Corps, England and it took only his serial number to get it to him…assuming the little broomstick and canvas airplanes had not flung him to the ground in a fit of rage.

Granddad had read that SA 5 was coming off the assembly line, and it was showing vast improvement. There might be an update possible on some of the earlier models. Good news, as long as it kept Wally safe either in the sky or on the ground.

He could have handed Rowenna's book to her in person, but better to wait for an address and mail it. Who knew how many possessions she was allowed. There was time....

He mailed the two books and brought the other one home. Mustard was still hanging his head, so Granddad made a trip to the paddock. Tossing a leg over the yellow horse, he guided him toward the mountain. Mustard whickered appreciatively over the effort, but his whicker was not as joyful as it could have been. Somehow Granddad and the horse were going to have to get themselves together. It could be a long war.

The short ride over, Mustard stood in the pasture and looked this way and that way. Nothing but birds and rabbits were moving. No girl. No jingle of harness. No fingers stroking his face. It could be a long war,

On the day the books were mailed, Wally stood before the SA 5 practically quivering with anticipation. The observer in the plane was in charge of a camera and must attempt to take enough pictures to give the generals an idea of what was going on...but the system was far from perfect.

A new plan was being devised. A particular type of camera was to be attached to the wing and operated from inside the aircraft. The camera, when in operation, snapped a shot every two seconds, and when developed, could be laid out in a connecting row and so much...SO MUCH...more could be determined. Distances could be more truly measured, and the pilot could fly with greater speed and, possibly, avoid more anti-aircraft fire.

And here he was standing by the first experimental plane. He would solo to the Iper River mouth, follow it to its first tributary branch and turn south to the Somme River mouth. By then his film would be gone, and he must head home.

A small side chore was requested. He must jog a bit to the south of the Iper River to the Tancrez Farm to see for certain if it was still safe. It was hoped that before the month was out that an aid station would be set up in the huge farmhouse.

At the correct time, Wally guided the four-spockited turning mechanism toward the Tancrez Farm. Hardly a minute later he flew over the huge + symbol painted in blazing red. Still there. Signs of a lot of activity. His camera shots should tell a lot.

Back to the Iper River he turned and followed it to the designated tributary and headed south to the Somme River. Even more activity. Motor launches were unloading supplies from a hospital ship. There were horses, a cannon, bales of what was probably supplies. Anyway that was not his concern. He had his mind on something else.

The Gotha Aircraft Factory in England had completed a biplane with two engines and a metal sheathing on the cockpit. It was set up to carry at least one bomb, and a tail gunner would be in charge of releasing the explosive when the pilot maneuvered into position. This plane was to have its maiden flight and a qualified pilot...maybe two...would be taken from the Royal Flying Corps for this test flight.

Would he...? Could he...? Oh, please, let it be him! This wonderful plane had only one fault, the extra wing. While it helped with lift, it was a bit heavy for only two engines. The engineers were sweating over a way to fix one or the other of the problems.

That, however, would not be the problem of 2nd Lt. John Wallace Hopkins of the Royal Flying Corp. "Oh, please let me test it?" he begged of the cloudless sky above him. What was that verse about getting the desires of his heart? It was a church marquee one time, and he and Rowenna had to scramble for enough letters, and he had to snug them close. Oh, yes...it was Psalm 37:4.

"Delight in the Lord and he will
  give the desires of your heart."

My angel...? Are you listening? Someone is going to be chosen to test that plane and no one desires it more than I do. Can you manage that...?

If guardian angels chose to speak, Wally's angel might have said, "Son, you have already been chosen."

SEPTEMBER 1917

It was now the fifth month after America had declared war against Germany and had prepared to combine forces her forces with her mother country, England, who desperately needed her.

England, though they should have seen events occurring, had remained hopeful that there would be no all-out war, and it was as though they attempted to bring this about by remaining unprepared. Consequently, when the war actually began, England began their preparation from a zero start while their enemy was at least a quarter of the way to the finish line.

Germany had developed undersea weapons they called U-boats (Undersea Boats) that could fight both under the ocean and on the surface. These boats had tubes like the barrel of a shotgun to shoot their torpedo bombs through the water at English shipping, and they had antiaircraft guns like high-powered rifles pointed to the clouds.

England had only their merchant ships and fragile aircraft… patterned after the toys of rich men's sons.

Granted, they made good speed when they got started, though it was mainly from the American Red Cross who put together the gifts of rich corporations and a few wealthy families, along with the blood and physical service of the sons of average Americans. The American Red Cross would now offer the blood and service of their daughters, as well.

The Medical Detachment on the mouth of the Somme River on the French/Belgium border was being manned from strong, intelligent men from the American Midwest. Hastily put together buildings and necessary provisions made it possible for Captain Nathan Wilkinson, U. S. Army Medical Department, to bring his services.

Half a world away, thirteen young ladies in the white uniform of the Red Cross, and the blue capes and hats, stepped aboard the rail car of the Burlington Northern Santa Fe, preparing to go to the east coast. They would wait there until Mercy Ship

157

Number Two returned with American wounded. It would be re-outfitted and returned.

Also aboard Mercy Ship would be Captain Marlene Cravens, American Red Cross Nurse Corps. This thirty-one-year-old would be the escort and chaperone of the thirteen young Registered Nurses.

After boarding the BNSF locomotive, Captain Cravens sent Group Leader Nurse Moffat to an adjoining car to take care of a few routine details. This chore was also to give the captain a chance to furnish a few necessary words of explanation to the remaining twelve without the presence of their group leader.

"Now, I have not heard of one word said against Nurse Moffat as group leader, but I know young ladies, and sooner or later some of you will wonder, and then you will begin questioning each other as to how she was chosen. I will now explain.

"Nurse Moffat has, on two separate occasions, saved a life by the use of her weapon, and one of those persons she saved was herself. She has single-handedly nursed two patients through a contagious disease, has stopped a train robbery, and has even risked her life to save a special horse that did not belong to her. She has assisted in more than a dozen childbirths, and she single-handedly delivered her sister of pre-mature triplets. She has six months of experience in stitching wounds and even setting bones when there was no higher expertise. She put herself through the nurse's training course, took the same test you took, and was awarded Gold Certificate.

"I am aware that each of you have certified with excellent grades, but that was not the final criteria by which you were selected. You were chosen for your various additional skills, and, most importantly, your brave willingness to be chosen. You will be doing many things that are not nursing, because you will have to eat and sleep, have clean clothes and keep your medicine cabinet ready. You will have many duties. There will be times you may have to protect yourself. In all of these occasions, you will work together...or you will not, actually cannot, be retained. I don't mean to scare you unnecessarily, but where you are going it is very dangerous and you are safer when you are together."

The twelve white-uniformed listeners were faintly pale of face. The captain had given them a lot to think about. As the captain paused and looked around for questions, the door opened and Nurse Moffat entered.

"Excellent timing," her captain commented. "I was just about to tell all of you what you would be doing while waiting for the ship. You will be issued a 9mm Walther handgun, and we will be learning how to take it apart and put it together, just as the soldiers do. You will learn how to clean and care for it and, while we are onboard the ship, you will be doing some target practice. Your skill may, and likely will, save a life and it will likely be your own."

She paused and a hand shot up. She looked into the sparkling dark eyes of Susan Spotted Pony. "Miss...uh, Captain, are you saying we can have our OWN gun? My brother has one and he let me shoot a few times, but he said the ammunition was too expensive for me to practice with. I didn't get a chance to get good. I already decided when I got a job that was the first thing I was going to get!"

Katie Campbell was next with the waving hand. "I saw a picture of one but it cost a lot of money. Will we really learn to shoot? Every one of us?"

Rosie Coyote clapped a hand over her mouth and giggled like a ten-year-old. "Oh, I can't wait! I wish we could have them now!"

The others looked from one to the other, and then at Rowenna. She could only smile and shake her head. "I've never touched one and I may be even more excited than you."

"When did you learn to shoot?"

Rowenna looked at the captain, questioningly.

"I told them you had experience with a gun, but I didn't say what kind."

Back toward her group she explained, "My granddad taught me when I was ten on a 22mm Winchester. I lived in the woods

159

and he thought the woods were dangerous. Actually, it turned out that they were."

The captain took a seat and listened to the chatter. Then, quietly she arose and went to the door of the railcar, and just before she closed it, she heard Rowenna comment. "You know, I have twelve brothers and sisters, but I have never felt more at home with them than I do right now."

Captain Cravens paused with the door somewhat ajar. There was a moment of silence until one after the other expressed a similar feeling. The escort smiled to herself and closed the door quietly. Whoever made the choices just from pieces of paper chose the Group Leader well. She's a leader without knowing it… just does and says what she must, and others respond. So far… so good!

If angels were in the habit of responding to the thoughts of humans, a group of them might have agreed…"so far…so good," but the beginning has not yet started.

On the other side of the world, the waters of the English Channel were at high tide when the cargo chip, City of Swansea, skirted the shore of Britain hoping for safety. The channel was known to be risky but so many important miles and days of time would be saved by using the channel and the cargo of coal must reach the French city of Bacou as soon as possible. The risk seemed worthwhile.

Of the many places England was not prepared to defend herself was under the sea, and the German U-boats totaling 200 feet and longer, plied the water like a school of sharks. The English Channel was also dangerous for the U-boats due to loss of maneuvering room but the benefits were tremendous. All Allied ships in the channel would be loaded with personnel or supplies, or something else valuable, and the cargo ships had even less maneuvering room than the U-boats.

The manned lookout points on the chalk cliffs of Dover, England, kept a constant watch over the channel for the dreaded submarines, but fog and rough water off the North Sea often made accurate sighting difficult to impossible.

All of this was known by the captain of UB 32 as it nosed its cigar shape bravely into the channel from the north. Ober Lieutenant Benno von Ditfurth, felt brave, having just received the Iron Cross 2nd class from his government, and he decided to take the chance. Sinking a cargo of coal was a prize and would see him in excellent position when the hated English were finally conquered.

For better vision, the U-boat commander brought his submarine scope out of the water for a position sighting just when the scope of the Dover lookout point passed over that section of water. The lookout commander blinked and took another look just as the scope lowered into the waves. Had that been a ripple from debris...? Better not risk it. Better to be ready than wrong.

The biplane D.H. 2, loaded with its one bomb, was brought into position and its propeller set to circling. The lookout commander strained his tired eyes. Was it? Wasn't it? False alarms were expensive and wasteful of their limited aircraft. But, yes... it had to be. There was the tell-tale pattern of deep waves on the surface of the channel.

He gave the signal and the current position of the sighting. It was a GO!

On the banks of the Somme River the barges were unloading the supplies he would need. Captain Nathan Wilkinson tensed with a shiver of nerves as he looked out over the English Channel, its small craft busily going here and there like so many water bugs.

The cargo ship City of Swansea was hugging the shore as much as possible as it squatted low in the water. Heavily loaded, obviously. As he watched the ship lumber its way along the busy shoreline, it suddenly erupted in a flash of fire, a boom that jarred the very soil beneath his feet and a billow of black smoke arose over the cargo ship. The channel water erupted into a thousand tiny waves, shivering their way to the shores.

Billow after billow of black smoke arose, each cloud seeming to be darker than the one before it. A tongue of flame burst through the deck, scattering a hundred small flames. Several explosions followed, and the whole ship began to list. All small watercraft scattered as quickly as possible against the suction of the sinking load of coal.

Staring with fascination, Captain Wilkinson watched the scene while those unloading supplies went about their business as though this was an everyday thing. Maybe it was.

On the Dover cliffs, the engine of the biplane screamed in anticipation as Captain Blue Thunder slammed his sizeable frame into the cockpit and Captain Hopkins positioned himself into the crowded bomb-bay. On signal from the ground, the wheels rolled and lifted, clearing the ground of the landing field.

Out over the cliffs and above the channel the new D.H. 2 roared, its engine on the max. Looking down from above, it was possible to see the movement in the water outlining the U-boat's shape. It even appeared to be rising again. Somehow, it must have seemed safe to the commander to take another satisfied look at his kill.

The first circle of the plane was out of position so it doubled back over the water at a point where the channel was seventy miles wide. Lots of room. Sharp turn and the pilot was in a better position.

This maneuver was something that the old SA 5 aircraft could not have done, but this baby was a dream to handle. Captain Blue Thunder's large hands caressed the steering mechanism fondly. This one could be a winner. Just add another engine and get rid of that top wing.

Sound from behind, faint over the engine and the wind. Instructions from the gunner. "Back off and dip!"

Captain Hopkins was ready...saw the hated pattern below him like some giant cigar...smiled and sighed with satisfaction.

He chided himself. *Don't get in a hurry. Wait...wait...NOW!*

The pilot felt the weight of the bomb leave his machine and he pulled up and turned, nose pointed toward the Dover Airfield. He couldn't resist another small circle...and both pilot and gunner saw the satisfying plume of smoke from the wreckage. Turning back they felt the rocking turbulence of air as the flame reached the U-boat's fuel supply and exploded into an oily shower of debris.

Items of lighter consistency flew away from the U-boat as it sunk lower. Its brave and successful commander, von Ditwirth, held to the wheel and stayed in his position until the water of the channel gushed in and claimed his last breath. He might have jumped to safety, but what glory would there be in that? For if he had, there was a more than even chance he would be picked up as a prisoner, and this way he would go down in glory with his ship.

One thing he knew without a doubt…his country would just as soon he go down. He had gambled and lost, and he bravely took his punishment. As the iron shark settled gently into the rubble and debris on the channel floor, he was gone. His country would fight on without him, but his sons could be proud of their father's great kill record, and perhaps they would be in the army that eventually conquered the hated English.

Captain Nathan Wilkinson heard the boom that took out the U-boat and he saw the smoke. The submarine had disappeared. He drew in his breath and looked around as the laborers continued to set up Somme River Medical Aid Detachment. What a life! Would he ever get used to it!

He turned and picked up a box of something that was undoubtedly necessary to his future and carried it to the enclosure that had taken shape practically before his eyes. This would not be the first time his hands and feet would operate without the conscious guidance of his mind.

The aerial team, Blue Thunder and Hopkins, settled the wheels of the D.H. 2 back onto the airfield and turned it over to the mechanics. They had just killed at least fifty men and buried them under the water of the English Channel. Once again Gunner John Wallace Hopkins reminded himself of what Granddad had told him. "Son, thou shalt not kill…unless it's either him or you. Then be sure to make it him."

I made it him…Granddad. Just like you taught me.

The cargo ship was in a shallow part of the water and had sunk barely below the water. Men came streaming out of stairways and, grabbing a life preserver, they swam to shore. No human losses, but the precious coal was spilling out onto the channel floor through the gaping hole in the ship's hull.

When the tide returned, some of the coal would begin its slow journey, being pushed toward the shore. Much of it would eventually be picked up by a householder for his home fires.

Back on the east coast of America the Red Cross ship, Mercy Two, appeared on the horizon. She would dock in the morning. Seven wounded men and 22 boxes, size 6x2 and flag-draped, were aboard and would be off-loaded with honors.

Captain Marlene Cravens grabbed newspapers as soon as they were printed. She searched the latest information from the English Channel and the Iper Salient, heavily aware that she was taking thirteen of America's precious little girls into the worse danger of their young lives…a place where their brothers already were.

And Captain Cravens had not yet heard of the sinking of the City of Swansea or the killing of submarine UB 32, and it was possibly just as well. (She was having enough trouble sleeping as it was.)

Granddad bought the latest papers and searched for the bad news, torturing himself, but having no power to stop it. *Dear God…send your angels and forgive me if I ask you to double the force.*

If angels desired to respond to humans, they might have reminded the tired, old minister to recall….

"…Yea, though I walk through the valley…of death, I will fear no evil…" (Psa. 23:4).

The light of his life had flown beyond his reach, and he could only pray for a happy landing as he watched the sunset over the mountain and ridge road.

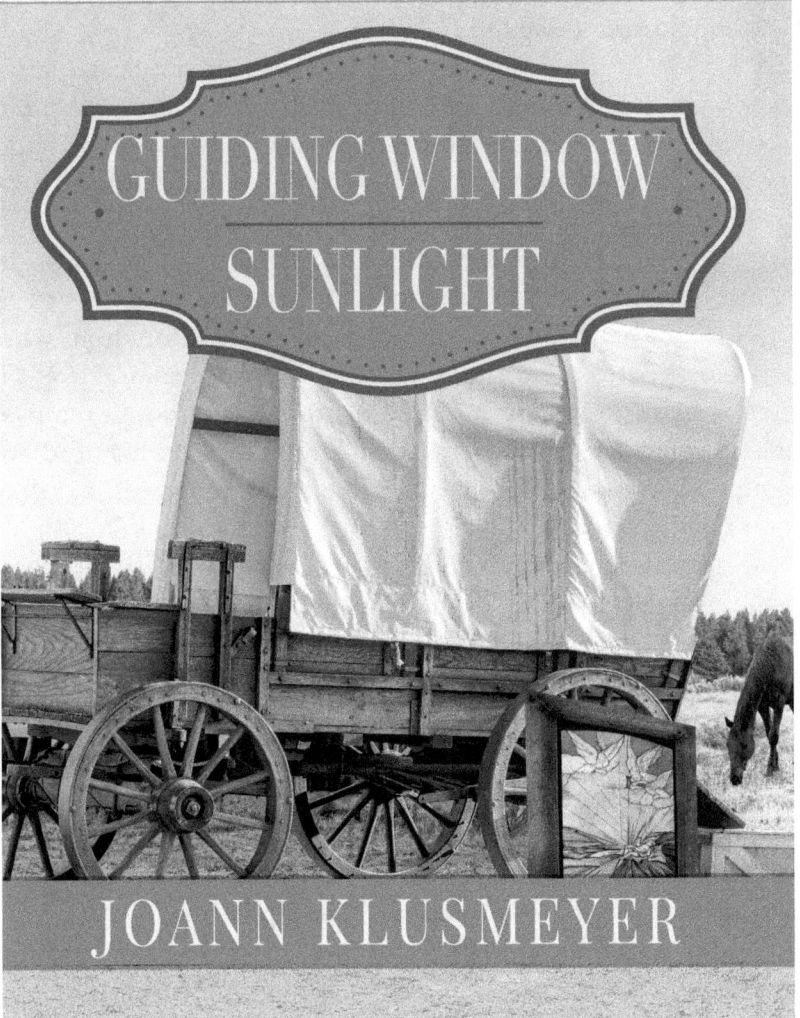

2

Taming the Wilderness Historical Fiction Series

GUIDING WINDOW
SUNLIGHT

JOANN KLUSMEYER

GUIDING WINDOW

ONE

G od told you to WHAT?"
Kathleen Palmer stood with her soapy hands spread apart in amazement as she stared at her new husband of six months. Her rosy red-gold curls had been pushed back with her sudsy hand, leaving a glob of white foam on her forehead. The clump of foam was sliding, unnoticed, down toward her lovely pink ear.

Hapgood Palmer, new husband, sighed and began again. He had known it would be this way. He had tried every way to get out of it, but he had no better luck than many before him, when they had tried to get out of a direct command from above. No amount of ducking away or attempts to move sideways removed him from the direct command that came down on his head and resounded around within himself, like the water wheel that drew water for the cattle.

He had repeatedly explained to God that He was talking to the wrong person.... as had Moses and Gideon before him. He explained to His maker that it was surely a case of mistaken identity, but God had not been successfully convinced and remained stubbornly adamant, succinct, and well centered with His wishes. Just as He was with Gideon and Moses. His attention was absolutely not to be drawn aside by a mere mortal.

The young man knew, however, that his wife deserved the best explanation he could give her. He began, "There don't seem to be no way to git around it. I got'a be a preacher."

Kathleen expertly stripped the foamy suds from her hands, flinging it into the tub containing her embroidered unmentionables, still bright and pretty from her bridal trousseau.

She wheeled around on her shapely barefoot heel and led the way from the washtubs of wet clothes to the door of the mountain cabin. This news was clearly something that should be taken sitting down and with full attention.

Hapgood, usually called "Hap," brushed back his coal black hair with a nervous hand and followed her.

Plopping herself onto the handmade wicker settee, she demanded, "Now, tell me again. Just exactly what was it that went on 'tween you and God?"

Hapgood, not feeling that he deserved to sit on the settee beside her, at least until this new directive from above had been absorbed, settled for a low stool at her feet and planted himself tentatively upon it.

"Lena, honey, don't think I ain't been a'tryin' to get away from it. I know what it's like bein' a preacher… livin' with one in the family I did. I know what it's like on the preacher's wife, and her bein' the innocent party to it all. Learned it all watchin' my ma. I talked to God, and I talked to God, and Him not seemin' to care how I feel about it all. Didn't notice that he took much notice's you, either."

Kathleen bent her lovely head forward and studied her toes, slightly muddy from the slopped over wash water and the rich, black dirt of the mountain farm. "You sayin' to me that this ain't a new thing to you? That you been hidin' all this from me? Now, Hap, you know we promised to not do that." The rebuke was gentle, but firm.

Hap had remembered. It had been easy to promise anything to the beautiful Kathleen O'Keen. The best day of his life was when he had stood in the parlor of his parent's house and promised to love, honor and protect her… and that was all he wanted to do, but there was no way to protect her from this. They were clearly in it together.

"Lena, honey, I wasn't in no hurry to talk to you, thinkin' it could be that I misunderstood what God was a'sayin' to me. I kept hopin' and hopin' I misunderstood."

She studied him for a moment. "How could a body misunderstand God?" Kathleen studied his pleading, open face, with a puzzled frown on her own.

Hap sighed, long and knowingly. "Ain't hard to misunderstand what God says if He's a'tellin' you to do somethin' you don't feel capable'a doin'. Wasn't hard at all."

Kathleen still struggled to understand. "Why'd you not be feelin' capable'a doin' what you was told to do?"

With a sigh, he began. "Well, I ain't studied, and I..."

Kathleen interrupted, "I 'spect they was a time your pa hadn't studied, neither. Wouldn't that be right?"

"Yeah. That was one'a them things I thought of."

Kathleen pressed unmercifully forward. "What was the other thing?"

"Huh?"

"The other thing you thought of? What was it?"

He sighed. "Gideon, in the Bible. About him bein' a farmer and God told him he was gonna have to be a general in the army. He didn't believe God, neither, and wanted a sign. 'Member, how he put the wool fleece in the bowl and asked God to make the fleece wet with dew and the grass dry? God did, and Gideon still wasn't sure, so he asked God to make the grass wet and the fleece dry and God did that."

"You sayin' you put out a fleece to God?"

"Yeah, you might say."

"What was it?" she demanded.

Hap hesitated. "Aw, Lena..."

"Tell me!" his wife demanded more sternly.

"I said to God if'n you didn't start in a'cryin' when I told you, I'd take it for a sign, for sure, that I hadn't been hearin' wrong. You bein' in the middle'a makin' baby things, like you are, I figgered cryin' was a cinch. Figured that'd give me the perfect out."

"You was expectin' me to cry? About words you was hearin' from God?"

"I thought it might be an even chance."

The girl nodded with understanding. "You wanted me to cry, to let you out'a doin' God's will."

"Well…" he hesitated, painfully. "I wouldn't put it like that, exactly. But they was another thing I thought of."

"Let's have it."

He summoned his courage and began, "You know, Gideon, he put out two fleeces to God. I only gave God one chance to back out'a callin' me. God ought'a be given another chance, wouldn't you think? Could be He's changed his mind."

Kathleen nodded, slightly, and turned her gaze out of the cabin door. Her white teeth caught her lower lip, as they often did when she was thoughtful. The color of her eyes turned from the pale blue of the summer sky to the deep swirling slate blue of a Kentucky mountain lake.

Hap waited. Ever since they were children in school, this color change had often brought on an idea. Some good, some not so good, but a thoughtful idea, just the same. It seemed to be worth the time, waiting to see what came forth.

"Now, Hap, I know the Bible didn't say nothin' about no Mrs. Gideon, but since this here thing affects me, too, I'd think it was fair if I was to get to put out the second fleece."

After a slight hesitation, Hap nodded. Why not? Seemed only fair, all right, and that'd put some of the responsibility on her.

Kathleen nodded and continued, "I want God to give us a sign so powerful that we know we didn't make no mistake. That'd seem fair to ask, don't you think? And I want it to happen tomorrow, before noon."

"Before noon?"

"Yeah. Gideon asked for his fleece to be wet over night. Seems like it'd be fair for me to put a time on it?"

"And what'd that sign be?"

"What it can be is for God to decide. He'd know how to make it big enough that we didn't make no mistake about it. We'd just have to trust 'im on that."

Hapgood Palmer watched the tiny smile creep into the edges of his wife's lovely mouth, and he saw the sparkles dance in her eyes. Once more he was thankful for the gift of this lovely creature. As soon as she understood the problem, she shifted the responsibility of it neatly back onto the shoulders of God... where it belonged.

What was it that could possibly happen that would be so big, as to be unmistakable, and occur before noon tomorrow? Especially in the tiny log cabin perched on the Kentucky mountainside so far from any main road to anywhere?

Hap breathed a sigh of relief. He would never have thought of anything so wonderfully hard for God to do. Nothing of such great importance and no surprises ever happened on this mountaintop.

He reached out from the stool where he sat and clutched the two bare feet before him, still slightly muddy and pulled them toward him.

"Now, Hap, you be careful!"

"I am! You notice I didn't grab a handful'a that hair. I'm bein' careful on account'a there being two a'you." He did, however, tug gently on the feet until she was removed from the settee and onto his lap.

TWO

Kathleen's wash water had cooled considerably before she returned to it and rinsed her unmentionables, hanging them on the line to dry. But she spent some very thoughtful time beside the washtub, before her dresses, and Hap's overalls had spent their time on the rub board and were on the line beside the underwear.

Hapgood went back to his fence mending. If a fellow aimed to keep his hogs from wandering the mountains and getting long legged and skinny, he must be diligent with the fences and plug up the holes they rooted along the edges. Fence mending was good for thinking and he had some of it to do.

He had his plans. Good plans. He and Kathleen'd likely need to spend two, maybe three years here on the mountain, and then he'd sell out and be able to get something larger closer in to town.

This cabin was a nice place for two people. Nice, until they decided to go somewhere in rainy weather. The mountain roads, and especially the one leading up to his house turned slick as glass and ran red rivulets as the rainwater washed potholes into the clay. That was good, in a way, because it had made the cabin affordable. But, he reasoned, pigs weren't going anywhere, anyway, except to market. Humans would just have to deal with it.

Wintertime meant there wouldn't be much going, anywhere. There'd come a time when coming and going would be more important, like when their children would need to be educated.

He whistled a lighthearted tune as he drove stakes into the ground at the site of the latest hog wallow. He occasionally glanced over the fence at the noisy rooters. They were looking good, this batch of hogs. If he could just keep them penned up, and not out running off all their meat, he'd make a nice profit when they were sold.

With that, and the money from the sale of the wicker chairs and settees he made, he should be able to afford a nice place in town in a couple of years, three at the most. His plans were firmly set.

He circled the hog pen, checking for other rooted-out escape holes and moved on to another enclosure, also filled with grunting Hampshire sows. Their white hair was now dyed red with the mud from the wallow, but their characteristically patterned white "jackets" over the black body were still evident. He liked Hampshires. They put on weight very well, the boars were fairly even tempered... for a male hog, that is... and the little white jacket pattern made them look like they were dressed up. When they weren't covered with mountain mud, that is.

He had done all the right things, hadn't he? God had said in His book that the man who did not provide for his family was worse than an infidel. Well, he was not one of them. He was as prepared for marriage as any 21 year old, maybe better than most, and Kathleen's pa had been first to say as much.

As he headed back to the cabin, he walked through the patch of corn that he grew to feed the hogs. The shiny, flowing leaves on the cornstalks reached his armpits, just as they should this time of the year. Ears were beginning to head up all along the stalk. There would be corn kernels for weight gain in the hogs and plant stalks for roughage.

This spring's litters of baby squealers were beginning to put on weight, and his highly-bred sows were still young. Clearly, everything was working out, and it had seemed that God approved and was on his side.

Next spring...? Well, anyway, things were looking very good.

Now this...

THREE

The pitch of the Kentucky mountain, leaning toward the south, as it did, created a lovely, cool night breeze blowing up the mountainside. The white starched curtains at the wide cabin window moved with the force of it.

It would be so pleasant to lie in the bed in the mornings, now that Kathleen was over the worst of her sickness, but they had already heard the flap of the rooster's wings, preparatory to the morning serenade. What with the crowing of the Barred Rock roosters, the mooing of the jersey cow, and the scratching of the dog at the door, it seemed time to get out of bed. They were clearly outvoted.

Besides, it was almost light in the east. Sunrise came early on the hilltop.

Another thing. God had until noon to do or not do what He wanted to get done. After that, they could settle into their planned routine without any upsetting problems to concern them. Their baby would be born, the farm would be in better shape than when they bought it, and they would get a good price for it. Then they would move down closer to the valley and their parents and friends.

But now it was time to get up. The corn could use another plowing before it got so tall the horse couldn't get through it. That should probably be the duty for today.

Hap pulled on his clothes and followed Kathleen to the kitchen. It was a pleasure to watch her cook. In addition to the knowledge that good food would be served, watching it being prepared was akin to watching a pair of orioles in flight, dipping and spinning in their courtship dance. Or a doe running through the trees, her fawn at her side. Or maybe a squirrel bounding about on the tree limbs, so nimble its feet hardly seeming to touch the limb. The whole thing made him feel poetic.

She stood there at the stove, his Lena, stirring the oatmeal with one hand, while dumping biscuit ingredients in the pan with the other. Sliding the oatmeal aside, she moved the skillet over the flame and plopped in a dollop of bacon grease, followed by four thin-cut pork chops. Then, both hands joined over the biscuit mixing bowl, and in seconds, the doughy globs were formed, popped in their pan and shoved into the oven.

The pork chops, crisp and brown, were fished from the skillet with the long-handled fork and put into the overhead warming oven to stay the right temperature while the eggs were cooked. One hand skillfully broke the eggs into the skillet, while the other hand set the jelly and honey down from the cupboard above the stove.

Milk, honey, jelly, and butter came to the table. The eggs got turned. Silverware arrived, followed by bowls of oatmeal and plates of meat and eggs. Lastly, on came the pan of biscuits, the tops as evenly tanned as a jar of bee tree honey. Hap could have gone on to the barn and already had the milking done, but then he would have missed watching the breakfast preparation. That surely would have been a pure waste of lovely viewing… maybe even a sin of wastefulness.

With a flourish and a swirl of her apron, Kathleen seated herself in the sturdy cane-bottom chair, made by her husband, and bowed her head.

Hap's voice intoned, "Dear Lord, we thank you..."

He had just picked up a biscuit and opened it for the butter when a light rapping sounded at the door. He and Kathleen looked at each other with surprise. How did anyone get past the dog without it setting up a racket?

Kathleen whirled from her chair and went to the door. The old man on the porch tipped his hat and smiled a snaggle-toothed smile.

"Mornin' Miss..."

"Mornin' to you, Mister. You come to see my hu..."

"You're fine, Miss. I come a'askin'."

"Askin'?" She was apprehensive.

By this time, Hap had managed to put down his biscuit and join his wife at the door. If someone needed directions, then they were certainly and hopelessly lost because the mountain cabin was not on the way to anywhere.

"Help you, Mister?" Hap asked, politely.

"Yes, Son, you can. Me and my missus, here, we come about as far as we can go. She's ailin' and we're two days short'a our destination. She was sayin' if there'd be a body close by that'd let her rest on their porch, maybe stretch out a bit without the swayin' of the wagon, it'd be a comfort to 'er. Maybe an hour... or two. Then, if there was a bite to eat that could be spared, that'd get us on our way."

Hap looked quickly at Kathleen's worried expression. She had only cooked the usual amount for the two of them, but they had two pork chops each in their plates, untouched. There were always biscuits...

"You folks come on in. We was just fixin' to sit. Your missus in the...?"

"There in the buggy," he supplied.

"You needin' help..."

"Yes, Son. A little help with 'er, if you will. My old arms, they ain't so strong nomore."

Hap followed the old man to the buggy in the yard, and Kathleen surveyed the table. Sliding two of the pork chops onto fresh plates, she opened four more eggs in the skillet. Two more oatmeal bowls... there was plenty of it. She always made extra for the dog. Biscuits? ...enough. Jelly? ....honey? ...enough. Yes!

She peeped through the curtain and saw the old woman being guided toward the porch steps. So thin, she was, that she was practically skin and bones, and her claw-like hands shook with palsy. Oops! Better fry them eggs a mite longer. Them old hands would never manage runny yolks.

Then they helped her through the front door, and the old woman was even worse off than she had appeared to be through the curtain. Her skin was darkened with age, her teeth, nonexistent. Her sparse gray hair was wadded into an inept knot on her head.

She smiled her toothless smile and settled into the chair designated for her. Kathleen slid the hard-fried eggs onto the plates and set them in front of the old couple.

Hap, the comfortable host, instructed them. "Dig right in, folks. It's done been prayed over."

Even eating as slowly as they could, Hap and Kathleen finished before the old woman, and finally Hap had to excuse himself to take care of the bawling cow. After the milking, he carried grain and water to the buggy horse.

Kathleen tried to keep from staring, and wanted, more than anything, to offer to feed the old woman with her own steady hand, but she kept silent until the food was gone. Finally, the toothless mouth was gumming its last bite of biscuit.

"Honey," the old woman said, smiling at Kathleen. "You been so good, I hate to ask one more thing, but I ain't got use'a my hands like when I was young, and getting' my hair combed, it's right much of a chore. If you could comb...?"

"Sure. I can comb your hair for you." Whereupon Kathleen picked up her comb and stood behind the old woman's chair, relieved to have something to do to keep her eyes off the pain in the old face.

Drawing the comb through the strands of oily hair disturbed her sensibilities. "Ma'am, you want I should wash out your hair? Bein' on the road like you was…"

"Honey, if you'd do that, it'd be a blessin'."

Draping the thin old shoulders with a thick wedding-present towel, she dipped water from the reservoir and moistened the gray strands. Massaging gently with her fingers, she brought out the dirt and oil, rinsing it off by holding the old head with one hand, and pouring water through her hair with the other, catching it in the dishpan. She blotted off the moisture and swished the comb through the soapy water.

Gently pulling through the snarls, she combed the hair until it was silky dry, and then skillfully twisted it into a stylish figure-eight knot, securing it using a few of her own pins. It helped the old lady's appearance quite a lot.

The old woman again gave her a toothless smile. "Now, Honey, if I could rest a mite. Your nice front porch'd be good. Just a little rest to get away from the swayin'a the buggy."

"Oh, no, Ma'am, you got'a lay on the bed. It's a good bed. My ma and me, we stuffed that mattress ourselves. My ma, she keeps geese just for the feathers. Says, otherwise, she'd not bother with the worrisome, noisy things. Here, you come on in here." Kathleen grinned, conspiratorially, "Them geese do make right smart of a tasty Sunday dinner, though."

Insistently, she guided the old woman into her bedroom. "Your Mister, he could come, too. He could likely use rest the same time as you."

She helped the old legs to straighten out, then covered them with a wool afghan knitted for her by her grandmother when she was a little girl. It had rested for years in her bridal chest. She stretched it to cover the feet of the old man, too.

"Now, you just rest and I'll be quiet as I can. Maybe them old roosters'll shut up."

176

Slipping back to the kitchen, she dipped water from the reservoir but it wasn't very hot. She had used most of it for the hair wash. Stirring up the firebox, she poked in several sticks of wood. She brought a pail of water from the well and dumped it into the stove reservoir. While it heated, maybe she'd stir up a little cake. Yes, an apple cake. If the old couple could rest until dinner, it would be a good desert to send them on with.

When the cake was ready for the oven, the water in the reservoir was hot again, so she could wash the dishes. Thoughts bubbled in her head. How did these people get to the porch without the dog barking, and how did they get so far off the main trail? If they were two days from their destination, would the old woman even make it? They must not have any food with them, so when they left her house, she'd need to put in enough to get them where they were going. Disturbing thoughts niggled themselves in the back of her mind, but she shoved them aside.

So what would two days worth of food be? Boiled eggs, cornbread, biscuits, cake, butter, canned peaches (did they have a jar opener?), a baked sweet potato… they were good even served cold, and… Well, what else?

She found the right size basket and packed the food inside so it would be ready. She even took it out to the buggy and set it on the floorboard, so there would be no argument about taking it. She felt a tinge of regret that she would loose that particular basket, but Hap could make her another one.

Glancing around in the buggy, she was amazed that they had so little in the way of comfort. Actually, they had nothing. But they'd get where they were going in two days, and for certain, they'd have plenty to eat.

By then, it was ten thirty. What for dinner? Fried potatoes, ham, green beans, spiced apples, and the cake? Good enough.

By eleven, the old couple was stirring, and Hap came in wearing dirty overalls.

His wife held her nose. "Been wrestlin' them pigs agin?"

Hap grinned as he changed. "I like them Hampshires, but they're the stubbornist critters for rootin' under the fence, that was ever made by God. Or whoever it was that made 'em."

By eleven twenty, the four of them were at the table, once more.

"Where ya headed?"

"Uh, down Louieville way," was the noncommittal answer.

A slight hesitation. "Well, ya ought'a make it. Good weather."

FOUR

At ten to twelve, the old woman was settled onto the buggy seat, exclaiming over the wealth of food in the beautiful basket. At five to twelve, they waved goodbye and the buggy moved toward the gate.

Hap and Kathleen stood on the porch as a good host and hostess would, waiting until they were out of sight before going back into the cabin, but instead of pulling through the gate, the horse was reined in and turned around to come back to the house.

"Young man," came a call from the saggled-toothed mouth.

Hap walked out to the buggy.

"All I got to give you for the help is my thanks, bein' I got no money. But I got this other thing, been savin' it for the right person. Figger that person must be you. Reach around here back'a me, and get that box."

"Mister, you don't..."

"I know that, but you're the right person to have it. I'm sure of it. Lift it on up there. I'd help, but my old arms... There, Son, slide it on over. I figger you and your bride might like lookin' at that, and time might come it'd mean somethin' to you. Be careful and keep it from bumps till it's opened. Wouldn't want it to break."

"Well, thanks... Mister."

"Don't mention it. God bless you."

Kathleen left the porch and joined her stunned husband who stood holding a box made of rough wood, about 3 1/2 feet by 4 1/2 feet, and only 8 inches thick. It was a bit heavy, as well.

"What ya got?"

"I don't know. Right now I'm tryin to figure where this was. There weren't enough room in the back'a that buggy for it. You can look at and see, it's too big for the space that was in that little old buggy."

Kathleen nodded, soberly. She, herself, had looked around, nosily, when she had loaded the lunch basket, and if the box had been there, she would surely have seen it. It was now twelve o'clock.

Taking the box to his workshed, Hap carefully lifted the shiny new nails and pulled the boards apart. Inside was a window… heavy glass… made of several glowing colors. He carefully lifted it from the box and held it up to the light. The Kentucky sun shone its light through the prisms of colored glass and created a picture of a baby lying in a manger. Each new color of glass was piped in a thin casing of lead. A lot of work went into making this picture.

Splinters of golden glass created the hay in the manger, and a silver halo crowned the baby. Far away into the blue sky, tiny angels of white glass filled the heaven. A slight movement of the window, and the angels seemed to move. The rough stones of the stable were each a different shade of brown or gray, and the white covering over the baby seemed to have sparkles captured within the glass.

It was just too beautiful for words, and they stared at it, until seven minutes after twelve.

Hap tilted his head to view the picture from a different angle. "This here's purty enough to go in the parlor… when we get one."

Kathleen was silent.

- END OF EXCERPT -

ADDITIONAL BOOK SERIES BY JOANN KLUSMEYER

The Great I Am Bible Story Series for Kids
6 books

The Young Pioneers Adventure Series for Kids
5 books

The Wentworth Triplets Mystery Series for Young Teens
3 books

Footsteps in the Canyon Adventure Series for Young Teens
4 books

Burnt Tree Junction Historical Fiction Series for Adults
6 books

Ozark Mountains Historical Fiction Series for Adults
7 books

Taming the Wilderness Historical Fiction Series for Adults
4 books

The Sheltering Stones Historical Fiction Series for Adults
5 books

The Trilogy of Wishbone Hollow Historicial Fiction Series for Adults
3 books